CLAIR

Beach Brides Series

Grace Greene

Whatever the season ~ it's always a good time for a
love story and a trip to the beach.

Emerald Isle, NC Stories

CLAIR

Beach Brides Series

Grace Greene

Kersey Creek Books
P.O. Box 6054
Ashland, VA 23005

Beach Brides (series name)

Cover Design by Raine English
Elusive Dreams Designs ~ www.ElusiveDreamsDesigns.com

Trade Paperback Release: May 2017
ISBN-13: 978-0-9968756-7-7
Digital Release: June 2017
ISBN-13: 978-0-9968756-6-0

Dedication

This book is dedicated to romantics everywhere, including the ones who have a book in hand and beach sand underfoot, whether in fact or in their imagination.

Introduction

Grab your beach hat and a towel and prepare for a brand-new series brought to you by twelve *New York Times* and *USA Today* bestselling authors...

Beach Brides! Fun in the summer sun!

Twelve heartwarming, sweet novellas linked by a unifying theme.
You'll want to read each one!

BEACH BRIDES SERIES (Clair)

Twelve friends from the online group, Romantic Hearts Book Club, decide to finally meet in person during a destination Caribbean vacation to beautiful Enchanted Island. While of different ages and stages in life, these ladies have two things in common: 1) they are diehard romantics, and 2) they've been let down by love. As a wildly silly dare during her last night on the island, each heroine decides to stuff a note in a bottle addressed to her "dream hero" and cast it out to sea! Sending a message in a bottle can't be any crazier than online or cell phone dating, or posting personal ads! And, who knows? One of these mysterious missives might actually lead to love...

Join Meg, Tara, Nina, Clair, Jenny, Lisa, Hope, Kim, Rose, Lily, Faith and Amy, as they embark on the challenge of a lifetime: risking their hearts to accomplish their dreams.

This is Clair's story....

For Clair Bennett, will her message in a bottle bring her the antidote to heartache, or the bad fortune that allows the man who broke her heart to hurt her yet again?

Find all of the Beach Brides at Amazon!

MEG (Julie Jarnagin)
TARA (Ginny Baird)
NINA (Stacey Joy Netzel)
CLAIR (Grace Greene)
JENNY (Melissa McClone)
LISA (Denise Devine)
HOPE (Aileen Fish)
KIM (Magdalena Kilmer)
ROSE (Shanna Hatfield)
LILY (Ciara Knight)
FAITH (Helen Kilmer Taylor)
AMY (Raine English)

CLAIR

Clair Bennett vacations in the Caribbean at Enchanted Island with her friends from the Romantic Hearts Book Club. While there, they each put a message in a bottle and then toss them into the Caribbean. Clair joins in the fun, but she isn't looking for love because she's already found her heart's desire. She and Sean Kilmer are engaged. She's eager to return home to Virginia where they're building a life together—until they aren't, and Clair is left wondering what went wrong.

Ten months later...

Stuck with the bills and repeated calls from creditors, Clair flees to Emerald Isle, NC where her sisters live. Her older sister has just dealt with her own heartbreak and her younger sister is traumatized by the loss of their parents. Clair feels caught in a tragic situation and it doesn't seem to be getting better until a stranger comes to town.

Greg Prescott has secrets, too, and he has his own reasons for coming to Emerald Isle, but he and Clair make a special connection and he may have to rethink his plans. Will Greg be the spark that helps the Bennett sisters begin to heal and find happiness again?

For Clair, will Greg be the antidote to heartache, or the bad fortune that allows Sean to hurt her yet again?

Prologue

~ Clair's message in the bottle ~

Clair Bennett
ClairIsAlreadyInLove@....

Chapter One

June ~ At Enchanted Island in the Caribbean

EVERYONE WAS HIDING something. Clair Bennett knew that was true for her, and didn't doubt for a moment that it was true for each of her friends. Even the most open among them had something to hide, whether scary or joyful, and one's first instinct was to protect oneself. Smiles could be genuine yet still serve as camouflage.

Who was it that first suggested they each put a message in a bottle and toss them into the Caribbean Sea? She couldn't recall. It seemed a silly gesture at the time. At first Clair dismissed the idea, but some of the gals were so excited about it, each imagining their dream of a guy, a sweetheart who'd come into their life and make it worth every heartache that had gone before. She couldn't say no. She felt a little dishonest pretending she, too, was still in search of love, but she didn't want to dampen anyone else's enjoyment, so she played along.

One of the gals gave her an empty bottle. Her friend, Lisa, gave her a pen. Clair saw a small card someone had left on a nearby table and she took it. She didn't need much writing space. Nothing would come of this stunt anyway, she thought, as she wrote her name on the blank card. In fact, she made sure of it by adding a fake email address. No phone number and no physical address—no crazy stranger could contact her. At the last moment, she realized there was raised lettering on the other side of the card. She flipped it over.

A business card from an attorney. She laughed. She didn't need a new boyfriend and she didn't need a lawyer either, thank goodness.

Clair laughed again as they launched their bottles into the sea and didn't give it another thought. As much fun as she was having with her friends, she was ready to go home to Virginia. That's where her fiancé and her future waited. She and Sean Kilmer were building a business and a life together, and that's where her heart was.

Chapter Two

April (Ten Months Later) at Emerald Isle, NC

CLAIR DREAMED THAT dream again. It didn't replay every night but often enough to make her apprehensive each time she surrendered to sleep. In her dream, the warm, dry grains of sand shifted beneath her bare feet. The onshore ocean breeze caught in the full skirt of her satin gown and the lace trim teased the soft flesh of her shoulders and neck. The pure white gown reflected the sunlight, as did the water a few yards distant. Together, they nearly blinded her, so she kept her eyes down, focused on the red bouquet clasped in her hands, waiting to hear The Words. The red flowers were echoed on her manicured nails against a white base, and all that red and white was repeated in the gowns of the bridesmaids, the bling in their barefoot sandals, and in the scattering of rose petals around them. Finally, she looked up, blinking against the reflected light, only to find herself alone. Alone. There was no one to perform the service, no bridal party, and no groom. Suddenly great drops of water fell from a gray sky and marred the gown. At that point, as always, Clair struggled to wake, gasping when she found herself back in her moonlit childhood bedroom.

She was crying. The wet blotches on the dream satin weren't rain, but tears. She had reason to cry. Her heart had been broken and she felt it rip again each time she had to deal with the aftermath of the breakup. Everyone had been sympathetic, including the rental hall, the caterer and DJ—though they'd all refused to refund her deposits. The house she and Sean had rented together, the utilities and other expenses...Sean had been busy with the business so she handled the wedding preparations and non-business commitments. Her name had been on those agreements. Plus, she'd loaned Sean money for the business. Not official loans because they were in this endeavor together and in love, so there was no proof. Proof didn't matter anyway. There was no money left and no Sean.

Her name hadn't been on the business debt. For that, she was grateful.

Nine months after the breakup she needed healing, not more sympathy or empty words, and she'd never wanted pity. She believed her dream wasn't really about the canceled wedding, but rather an expression of grief for the loss of everything she had worked for, including what should have been the celebration of the business and the future she and Sean had built together.

Every hope had turned into lies and betrayal.

The loss of her real-life dream had been a shock. But continuing to dream of it or to regret it was foolish. Yet it kept coming back, bleak and unresolved, like the current state of her life.

Clair dragged herself out of bed, peeked in on Darcy—still asleep—and headed to the kitchen, following the promising aroma of caffeine.

Her sister Mallory was already dressed for work in a suit and low heels. She was pouring coffee into her travel cup when Clair walked in.

"Morning," Mallory said.

Clair admired her older sister. Mallory always looked so together. Clair didn't have that gift. Mallory's dark hair was close-cropped and sleek. Her clothing never wrinkled or got food-spotted. Clair ran her fingers through her own long, curly brown mop of bedhead hair to get it out of her eyes.

"You're up early," Clair said.

"Early start for an early showing." Mallory secured the lid on the cup. "These clients may tie up my whole day. I don't know what time I'll be home. Hopefully, for supper."

"Okay." Clair wasn't a morning person. She struggled to shake off her fuzzy brain state. It had been a rough night. The back door was already open. Through the screen the promise of a beautiful spring morning sailed in on a fresh breeze. One couldn't see the ocean from here, but the salt air riding the onshore wind mixed with the usual coastal smells, and made its proximity unmistakable. She loved this place. All of it. The Outer Banks, the Crystal Coast, Bogue Banks, including this small bit of heaven that had been their parents' home. It was only a few blocks from the beach, and was nestled in its own small haven of Live Oaks and shade.

Mom and dad had been gone for more than three years.

Clair went to stand at the open door. The lavender-colored azaleas, the early bloomers, produced abundant blossoms. They were sheltered by an ancient, twisted, Live Oak. The yard was a mix of shrubby green stuff and lean, fine sand—a challenge for gardeners. Their parents had put years of effort into the landscaping and now nature was deconstructing it, reclaiming it. Neither she nor Mallory made any pretense of being gardeners. They hadn't tried to keep it up, not even her dad's roses. He'd made growing roses an art, always talking about protecting the plants from the ocean winds and the salt air while still getting good sun, and keeping the soil amended, moist, and mulched. The straggly, thorny branches framing dad's wrought iron bench were barely recognizable as rose bushes now. Last year, they'd produced hardly any blooms.

Standing at the door, remembering, she could almost hear his voice again, an echo from the past, humming or whistling as he tended the garden, or calling out to his daughters or their mom to come see the latest bloom.

The scent of her mother's rose sachets seemed to surround her. As far back as Clair could remember, her mother had collected the petals from the rose bushes and arranged them on cookie sheets and pizza pans to dry. Those pans occupied every flat surface in the kitchen for several days. After the petals had dried, mom added in spices like cinnamon, ginger and allspice, and then stuffed the mixture into small packets made of netting and ribbon. She hung them in closets and tucked them into drawers. The scent of roses that permeated their home had been a fact of life. Clair missed it. She suspected the same was true for Mallory and for their youngest sister, Darcy.

When their parents died, Clair was living in Virginia, working and falling in love with her boss, Sean.

She was eighteen years older than Darcy. Mallory, two years older than Clair, was working in the Raleigh area and dealing with a divorce. Darcy was only six at the time, a late arrival to the family. She had always been a shy child, and, in many ways, an only child since her sisters were so much older. Just a cute, quiet kid, who became quieter after losing mom and dad, until she stopped speaking altogether. There were days when Clair wondered whether their little sister would ever be able to grow up and leave home, have her own life and be her own person. Mallory always got angry when Clair tried to discuss that possibility.

"You okay?" Mallory asked.

Clair turned away from the door to face the room and her sister. Mallory held a mug of coffee toward her and she accepted it gratefully.

"How'd you sleep?" Mallory asked.

"Fine. It's just early. You're the morning person. Not me." She tried to end the sentence with a smile.

Mallory said, "I have to run. These clients could mean a big payday for us. Darcy is still sleeping." She stopped, a large leather business tote hanging from her arm, and fixed her gaze on Clair's face. "*She* had a restless night, too."

It wasn't an expression of complaint, but of

sadness.

After Mallory left for work, Clair closed the kitchen door despite the view and the tempting ocean smells, and locked it.

Poor Mal, having to deal with two restless dreamers—Clair was sorry to have disturbed Mallory's sleep because of her own inability to put the past behind her and move forward.

She checked on her little sister. Darcy was still in bed, rolled up in her covers like a cocoon. Clair eased the door closed and took the opportunity to grab a quick shower and to dress. As she stood at the sink brushing her teeth, she avoided seeing her reflection. A year ago, this wasn't where she thought she'd be now. She should've been in her own home, still a newlywed, enjoying life with Sean. Somehow, she'd screwed that up. Or Sean had.

She wanted to assign blame, to understand what had happened. But had never been given that chance.

Sean. Sean. She tested the sound of it, and yes, it hurt to think his name. After all these months, she should be past the pain. His name and memory should be no more than a tender spot she could sidestep with ease. But it wasn't.

Darcy's bedroom door was ajar. Her bed was

empty. The pillow lay on the floor and the sheets were awry. Clair hurried down the hall and to the kitchen, sure of where to find her. Her sister loved breakfast.

She was already seated at the table. Her long blond hair was a mess from the restless night. Her pajamas were twisted and wrinkled.

Clair smiled. She started their day with the usual greeting and question. "Good morning, Darcy. What would you like for breakfast?"

No response was expected. None was given. The question was pointless because the menu never varied. Cheesy eggs and toast with cherry jelly. No orange juice. Darcy wouldn't touch the stuff. She was a lemonade lover. She was almost ten, and though she was wordless, she was absolute about what she would or wouldn't do, including what she would and wouldn't eat. Usually cooperative, she balked when she disagreed with what was being asked of her, and when that happened no power or persuasion could move her.

Darcy had no words. She was plenty smart, though. Clair was certain of it. But if you were hoping for a smile or nod or a temper tantrum, you were asking for disappointment. Clair believed that one day all the words Darcy had been hoarding for three years would burst out. She was eager for that day.

Clair pulled the frying pan from the cabinet and fetched the egg carton and other items. She turned to her sister. "Darcy, can you set the table, please?"

Darcy selected a fork from the silverware drawer and returned to sit at the table. Clair observed the action, but didn't remark. Apparently, the table was now sufficiently set. Clair added plates and her own fork, then turned back to scramble the eggs and pop the bread into the toaster.

When their parents died, Mallory accepted the role of legal guardian and returned home to raise Darcy. Clair gave her credit for never suggesting she should also return to help. Mallory had packed up her personal life, including her career selling real estate, and moved. She said markets could be tricky, but houses were houses wherever they were and having grown up here, she felt confident. Mallory made it seem very convenient and logical because that's how she functioned. Later, Clair realized it was more than that. Mallory had never liked Sean. She would've known that involving Clair would likely involve Sean, too, and so she made the choice to shoulder most of the responsibility on her own.

Neither had believed their little sister would stay silent, or that school and other normal kid activities would be impossible for her. The doctors said Darcy was healthy. The therapists put a name to her condition, but that changed nothing. Mallory believed that their sister's wall—because it was a wall, invisible, yet as impenetrable as steel—would come down one day.

Mallory was a responsible, productive business woman who never saw failure as failure, but rather as a signal to try something else. Clair had returned home last August, about a month after the breakup with Sean. Until that time, Mallory had followed the therapists' instructions, including medications. All with no apparent change. About a month after Clair returned, Mallory said, "Enough. She's not a guinea pig. Let's give her time."

Clair had doubts. For months now, she'd seen Darcy's wall, securely in place, day after day. She feared her sister had settled into this silent state. That the love and support she received from her older sisters might be part of the problem. Were they enabling her? Could this become permanent?

Suppose her condition continued indefinitely? A trapped, panicky feeling rose in Clair.

In silence, Clair and Darcy finished their breakfast. She wanted to shake her young sister up, motivate her, do something to bring her back to herself, to make her want to return to them instead of shutting them out.

Clair stacked the plates and utensils in the sink and began rinsing them. Through the kitchen window, she caught sight of the azaleas again. Their bright color eclipsed those poor orphaned rose bushes. As her parents had loved their azaleas and roses, they'd loved their unexpected daughter much more, the baby who'd arrived after they thought their nest was comfortably empty. They had adored this child who was bright and beautiful—whose laughter and tears and words had been shut off like a faucet with their loss. Clair spoke aloud, raising her voice to be sure her sister heard her.

"Let's walk on the beach, Darcy. It's a beautiful day."

Darcy's chair scraped the floor. Clair turned. Her sister was already gone.

Clair always laid out Darcy's clothing the night before. Sometimes Darcy took the initiative, but more often, she didn't dress for the day on her own unless Clair insisted or provided incentive. A walk on the beach was incentive. Darcy donned her shorts and t-shirt within minutes and her favorite bucket, bright red, was already out on the bed, ready to go. Clair brushed her sister's hair and insisted she brush her teeth, then went to change into her own shorts. She tucked a light sweat jacket into her backpack in case it was breezy down by the ocean and added a beach towel. She fit in a couple of water bottles, too. Seemed like they did this nearly every day now.

Their home was situated two rows back. It was a three-block walk from the ocean—one block west, then two blocks south because the island of Bogue Banks lay east-west instead of north-south like the usual east coast beaches. They could walk or drive to the beach access lot. The lot only had a handful of parking spaces and you couldn't count on parking there in the summer season, but this time of year wasn't a problem. If they drove, and didn't get too sandy and wind-blown, they could stop at the grocery store on the main road before returning home.

In the car, Darcy's tight grip on the bucket handle betrayed her eagerness to go to the beach. Her expression was impassive, as usual, yet Clair imagined she saw expectation in her sister's posture.

Reality was cruel. Their mom had gone swimming and gotten into trouble. Dad left Darcy on the beach and swam out to help. They both drowned. People coming to enjoy the beach that afternoon found Darcy sitting on the sand surrounded by the toys and towels and stuff her parents had brought with them in the morning. She was quietly crying. All they could get out of her was that mama had called for help and daddy had swum out to her.

Their bodies weren't recovered for several days.

A reasonable person might assume the memory of the tragedy would cause Darcy to despise the ocean and avoid the beach, but this was the place she most wanted to be. Clair knew that in Darcy's head, the ocean and the loss weren't connected. Most likely, at the beach her sister felt closer to the happy times spent here with their parents. Clair wondered if her sister fully understood what had happened that day, or whether she had simply rejected the reality of it altogether?

Clair parked the car in the small lot. They walked along the sandy path between the shrubby growth and the wind barriers. Darcy carried her red bucket. Clair carried everything else. It was routine. It disturbed her. Was she here to assist with and care for her sister? Or to disappear into this half-life along with her?

Trauma. Stress. Whether it was physical or emotional, everybody had some experience with it and everyone handled it differently. Clair just wanted to collapse on the beach blanket and not think about anything except how to move on.

It was too early in the season for swimming and Darcy couldn't be trusted in the deeper water even if she was interested in wading, which she never was. Mostly she liked to play in the wet sand, digging a little or drawing in it. She rarely bothered with the shells and bits of sea glass that washed up with the tide, and never finished building anything recognizable. Simply, she seemed content to be near the ocean.

Clair settled on the blanket nearby.

If she had been here to witness the tragedy, she didn't think she could have forgiven the ocean for what it had stolen from them. When she was told the bad news, she'd clung to Sean in her grief. She remembered how he'd comforted her, and it tore her heart a little more. She pushed the memory away preferring to watch her sister playing in the sand, the sunlight glinting off her hair, absorbed in her quiet world.

Clair was curious about her sister's world, but no invitation to enter had ever been extended.

To honor memories and to honor life, one had to live well in the present. Live well and to the best of one's ability. Otherwise, what was all the past hurt and turmoil about? Why bother to be a survivor? She believed that, but it was still hard. She needed to focus on other things. New possibilities. She had to find a way to put the hurt caused by the loss of her parents back then, and that dealt by Sean last year, behind her.

It was a beautiful day at this nearly empty beach.

She retrieved her phone from the backpack intending to check her texts and emails. The picture on her phone screen showed a beach, but not this one. Instead, the bright sun, white sand and turquoise waters belonged to the beach at Enchanted Island.

The Caribbean trip had been nearly ten months ago, a year ago come June. Her online group, the Romantic Hearts Book Club, had planned it. They were all romantics who'd been hurt by love—not a great thing to have in common—but they also shared a love of books. Sean and she were in Virginia, working hard, and she hadn't been eager to go on the Caribbean trip. The timing was bad. Sean encouraged her to get away.

They'd been in his office reviewing his schedule when she noticed the big meeting with Tom Woodhurst, a potential investor, had been moved up on his calendar. Sean was promoting a new piece of equipment; a gadget was how she thought of it. The gadget was supposed to fit in a car's engine and make it work more efficiently and economically, in addition to improving emissions performance. Sean had spent a ton of money acquiring the patent, but was having difficulty getting it into production. They'd had a few expensive hiccups in the process.

Clair didn't understand how the gadget worked

its magic, but that was okay because Sean did, and she absolutely believed in Sean. She knew how important this upcoming meeting was. She just didn't know the timing had changed. Sean hadn't mentioned it.

"What about the investor, Sean? Don't you need my help when Mr. Woodhurst is here? To wine and dine him, and all that good stuff? Maybe field some of the business questions?"

He wrapped his arms around her. He assured her, "I've got it handled. No worries. He likes me, you know." Sean laughed, then became more subdued. "Seriously, Woodhurst trusts me." He kissed her cheek. "Besides, you work too hard. It'll do you good to get away and you don't want to let your friends down."

"I hear it's a beautiful island."

"Island. Caribbean." He danced her around the room as if hearing a calypso rhythm. "Hard not to be beautiful. Just like you." He stopped and kissed her.

She leaned her cheek against his shirt. "I wish you could go, too. Seriously, I'll reschedule and go with you instead of the girls. They'll understand when I tell them about our engagement."

"Now that's an idea, but why not go twice? You go now. Scout out the area and we'll go back on our honeymoon."

It was such a fabulous idea. She could enjoy her friends, plus it would be almost like Sean was joining in on the trip. She would call and send him pictures and take notes about what they could do there while on their honeymoon. She was imagining the possibilities when his phone rang.

She looked across the desk at the phone screen. "It says Dee. Who's Dee?"

"Who?" He released her to grab for the phone. "Deidre. She's Woodhurst's assistant. His daughter, actually. Probably confirming the meeting." Sean answered the call as he walked out of the room.

He was absentminded when on calls and often seemed to forget she was there. His voice faded as he reached the end of the hallway and the empty breakroom, then he turned, saw her watching him, and waved before turning his back again.

Clair had waited. If Deidre was only confirming the appointment, it should've been a quick call. It wasn't. It worried her. They'd reached a critical point in the business and Clair knew Sean was anxious though he tried to hide it. They needed fresh funding, so this meeting was critical. Despite Sean's encouragement, she almost canceled her trip. Finally, he was done with his call and rejoined her.

"Is everything okay?" she asked.

"Definitely. It's all good. Woodhurst wanted some product details for his technical people. It's all on track."

Reassured by Sean's upbeat attitude, she kept to her plans. A few days later she was in the Caribbean and grateful that Sean was such a thoughtful and understanding fiancé.

She was eager to share her good news with her friends, wanting to shout to anyone who'd listen that she was in love and had everything good to look forward to, but once she was at Enchanted Island and they were all face to face, it seemed wrong. Like bragging. Each one had had their share of hurt and she didn't want to make it worse by proclaiming that her lonely heart days were over. She decided to wait until after the trip. When they were all back home, flush with delightful memories, she would post about her engagement in their group online.

Clair's book club friends were so much fun. On the trip, they shared a lot of laughter and a few tears, too. And the pact. Now that was really silly, but sometimes silly was the best thing of all. Who had suggested the message-in-a-bottle idea? She didn't recall, but each had found a bottle that meant something to them, or not, but it was up to the girl. Clair had kept her own counsel except for a brief chat with Lisa. Everyone had written their names and email addresses on slips of paper, though some had written much more. They inserted the messages into the bottles and tossed them into the Caribbean.

Clair had felt a little guilty. It was like littering, wasn't it? Was that how sea glass came to be in the ocean and eventually wash up on beaches? She laughed, but not happily. Were there so many hurting hearts? Broken hearts with foolish hopes that they created enough sea glass for beachcombers to collect, and for crafters to create jewelry and mosaics?

Her own, secret joy hadn't lasted long after her return to Virginia and had never been shared with the group. Ironically, a month after she got home, Sean had left a message of his own, though not in a bottle. He offered no explanation, only a brief apology scribbled on a scrap of paper that ended with a request not to try to find him.

She avoided the online group. She couldn't bear to see that others were finding happiness. She wished them all love, but she didn't want to hear about it. Not yet. Maybe someday.

Physically and mentally back on the beach at Emerald Isle, Clair watched her sister take her bucket to the edge of the water. She held it there to catch the tip of a wavelet and then she ran back to her sand creation and poured water into a small ditch surrounding it. A moat, maybe?

"It's time, sweetie. Fill in the holes and rinse your bucket."

As usual, her sister didn't answer, but she did as she was asked. That was proof of something, whatever that was.

Clair shook the beach towel and stowed their items into the pack. They walked back along the path to the car. Next stop would be the grocery store. Darcy's shorts were damp. They were both a little sandy and wind-blown, but not too badly. Luckily, this was the beach. A little wind, sea and sand were perfectly acceptable accessories for daytime wear.

****

Clair paused at the front door. Her arms were full of grocery bags. She managed to unlock and open the door, and Darcy chose that moment to refuse to move. She made that expression—one of her rare expressive looks—with a vertical line between her eyebrows, and her lips pursed together while she stared at the floor. It meant she wasn't going to be persuaded. She'd been so cooperative at the store that Clair had stayed longer than usual and over-shopped—meaning she purchased more than she could carry at one time, yet keep a hand free for her sister. These bags were getting heavy. Darcy didn't carry bags. Only her red bucket.

"Fine, then. You can stay on the porch." Clair nodded toward the porch swing and waited while Darcy sat. "Stay on the porch," she repeated, loudly enunciating each word. It was a screened porch so there was a sense of security and boundaries. "Sit there and watch the last bag. Don't leave. I'll be right back."

Except for simple, daily routines in the house, her sister rarely initiated any action on her own, so there was little risk in leaving her on the enclosed porch for the minute or two Clair needed to take the bags inside.

She nearly dropped the grocery bags, but made it to the kitchen in time. She set them on the counter and groaned in relief, shaking her arms and rubbing the muscles. One more bag to go. The trip to the beach this morning had brought back too many memories. It had thrown her off her game.

She pushed away from the counter and headed back to the front door. As she stepped outside she saw the porch swing was empty. No Darcy. No bucket even. The last grocery bag was half-off the chair, torn, and its contents were scattered across the painted wood floor.

Clair's heart skipped a beat thinking of those ocean waves only a few blocks away. She jumped a box of cereal and several cans of green beans as she pushed past the screen door. It slammed behind her as she ran down the steps into the yard.

She didn't have far to go.

Darcy was standing in the road with a man. Clair did a quick assessment of the man and the situation. His car was stopped but not really parked. She guessed he'd braked abruptly and left the car aslant. The man, his dark hair cut close on the sides and longer on top, was dressed casually in khakis and a lightweight tan jacket. He was kneeling and speaking to her little sister. His posture seemed kind, not threatening. Darcy, still holding her bucket, stood relaxed in front of the man and Clair saw his expression change from serious to puzzled. He looked up, saw Clair approaching, and stood. She noticed he was holding a folded sheet of paper. He glanced at it and slid it into his pocket. Directions, maybe? Was he lost?

Her heart pounded. The guilt over losing track of her sister, however briefly, made her head buzz. She had to keep calm, both for herself and the situation, to ease this stranger's concern, and to not upset Darcy. There was always a fear that someone might complain to the authorities about the strange little girl who didn't go to school, didn't play with the other children, and who, by the way, was an orphan. She and Mallory were careful to make sure of the legalities like the guardianship, but Clair never quite trusted that some governmental agency wouldn't intervene and decide Darcy wasn't progressing as she should, especially since Mallory had halted the meds and the therapy sessions. The authorities might decide that Darcy needed more professional care than her sisters could provide.

Clair rested her hands lightly on Darcy's shoulders. She spoke courteously, forcing a smile onto her face. "Is everything okay?"

The man said, "Yes. She walked into the road. She seemed...unaware of the danger." He gestured toward the car. "I saw her and stopped in time."

"Thank goodness. I appreciate your help. Thank you." She grasped Darcy's arm to pull her away. She resisted. Clair took her hand instead and tried to cover the awkwardness with an explanation.

"She probably wants you to know she's sorry for alarming you." She touched her sister's chin and lifted her face so she could meet her blue eyes. "Darcy? We need to let the nice man get on with his day." Clair shifted her gaze back to him. "Again, I'm sorry for the inconvenience."

She liked his eyes. In them, she saw kindness. She liked the set of his jaw and his slight smile. She saw strength in his face, not to mention in his broad shoulders. Her assessment of him sent a brief rush of reassurance through her and warmed her. She hadn't perceived any positive qualities in men in quite a while. She chose to see this as a sign of her own recovery and she probably smiled more broadly because so did he. It was the perfect moment for a smooth, graceful withdrawal.

Darcy's shoes had somehow become glued to the ground. She refused to respond to Clair's gentle tugs. Clair was stuck, too. Darcy was almost ten, not a toddler she could pick up and jounce on her hip.

The man saw Clair's difficulty. "Is she okay?"

Okay had a world of meanings.

Clair paused, then said, "We had a tragedy a while back and she's taking time to recover. Otherwise, yes, she's fine."

The man stared at the child's sandal-clad feet before refocusing on Clair. He said, "Maybe she'll go if I walk with you?"

Such a strange suggestion. An unexpected offer. It surprised her, but she considered it. Any idea that might get them off the street and away from the prying eyes of neighbors had merit.

"We could try."

He touched Darcy's arm, smiled at her, received no apparent response, and yet she moved alongside him as he walked to the porch.

When they reached the steps, he stopped and seemed uncertain. His arms moved, his hands unsure where to settle, and then the awkwardness was gone. He offered Darcy his arm and they ascended the porch steps together. She moved like a princess, her fingers resting lightly on his jacket sleeve.

Clair stared, amazed. Where had she learned that? Darcy had missed the princess phase that most little girls went through...or had she? At any rate, once on the porch, he made no mention of the groceries on the floor, but simply knelt to pick them up. Clair did the same. Darcy perched herself on the swing, seemingly content to watch them. She'd released her bucket and it was now on the swing seat beside her.

"This behavior is unusual. Normally, she's very agreeable. She wouldn't wander into the road either...usually. Perhaps the falling groceries disturbed her? I was carrying the bags in and.... I'm sorry. I don't mean to ramble on." She stood and clasped her hands together.

"Not a problem. Really. I'm glad it all worked out." He nodded at Darcy and said, "It was a pleasure to meet you."

There was no response, of course, though today's small surprises might have encouraged Clair to hope for more. On the other hand, she had gotten out of the habit of expecting welcome surprises and who wanted the unwelcome kind?

Clair pushed open the screen door and indicated he should precede her down the steps. As they walked toward the street and his car, he said, "I apologize for asking, but what's wrong with her?" He rubbed his jaw. "I'm sorry, that came out sounding different than intended."

He stopped and stared into the distance. "I thought she was just oblivious to traffic and danger. I was annoyed, but then I realized there was more to it."

"She'll be fine. Thank you again. I'd better get her inside. She's had a busy morning."

"Of course. Time for me to go, too." He gave her a quick smile and went to his car.

Clair lifted her hand in an almost wave before catching herself. She hurried back to the porch to get her sister safely in the house and back on schedule.

Chapter Three

Greg

GREG PRESCOTT STRUGGLED with what to say to the woman when she rushed over to where he was speaking to the child. Her dark eyes were flashing and her hair, long like the child's but brown and curly, was blowing in her face. He wanted to ease away casually and leave with as little conversation as possible.

This was just a drive-by to double-check where she lived. He'd come a long way for a simple job—from California to Virginia. In Richmond, a former neighbor said Clair Bennett moved back home to her family in North Carolina. It had taken him almost as long to drive down to Emerald Isle as the flight had taken from California, but the weather was great and he'd done far more dangerous jobs in his life, so what was he complaining about? This was almost a paid vacation. That thought made him laugh. Really, he felt like he was taking money under false pretenses. In fact, he'd said as much to the client before agreeing to accept the job.

Fly cross-country to confirm a location? He advised the guy to hire someone local, had even offered to recommend an investigator who was already on site. Someone familiar with the area would make more sense. But the client was the kind of guy who got an idea in his head and couldn't let it go. Greg had seen that right away. When he showed up at the guy's house for the appointment and was shown to the pool, the man was set up at an umbrella patio table like someone new to the high life, feeling flush, and playing it up.

Greg knew who the house belonged to—one of the benefits of being local—and it wasn't this guy. While they were talking, a long-legged woman, model-thin and wearing expensive sunglasses and jewelry, walked out of the house like she belonged there. Which she did. He recognized her as the daughter of the owner.

He'd dealt with this kind of client before. A business-type with big ideas. Soft. Who thought he was tough and smarter than most, but who took offense easily if he felt diminished and went from self-absorbed to offended in a blink.

Greg tried to keep impatience out of his voice. "I can highly recommend some investigators already in the area. It will make more sense, be a lot more economical, than paying for me to travel to the east coast to—"

The man cut him off with a raised hand. After a quick glance back at the woman to ensure she was still out of hearing distance, he asked, "Do you want the job or not?"

So, yeah, Greg said he did. A paying job was a paying job and the guy was footing the expenses.

He handed Greg a folded paper. Greg checked it. "This is her name?"

"Yes, but don't contact her. I don't want to make her suspicious or anything. I don't want to draw her attention if she isn't already...you know. Aware. I just want to know where she's at and if anything looks...well, just tell me where and what."

"Does she have family or friends she might go to?"

"Sisters in North Carolina, on the beach. No one else that I know of."

When Greg agreed to take the job, the client visibly relaxed. He babbled on for a few minutes, telling some stupid story about an island and a bottle. An *empty* bottle which, if on vacation in the Caribbean seemed pretty useless to Greg. He listened, tried to appear interested, and left as soon as possible. The guy, in fact, this whole job, smelled like a nuisance from the start.

Greg knew he would do a lot better as an investigator, professionally, if he had a higher tolerance for client B.S.

But he'd come here, found her, and had done as asked except for making contact. He hadn't intended to do that, but it was okay because it couldn't be avoided and he'd minimized any potential for damage.

Not that he could really take credit for the lack of chit-chat there on the street and on the porch. The woman, Clair Bennett, had been so concerned about getting the little girl away and into the house without a fuss, that she never questioned why he was there. She assumed he almost hit the child with his car, but there hadn't been any real danger. He'd already slowed almost to a stop as he was surveilling the house. The child left the porch and came directly over. For reasons he didn't understand, she bee-lined straight across the yard and to the road and to him. He'd waited and didn't know why.

He hadn't planned to speak with her. Not to Ms. Bennett or the kid. An almost eerie child. Pale with long blond hair, and with a look on her face...not blank as he first thought, and maybe serene rather than eerie? Made him think of Alice in Wonderland. A girl on an adventure of her own and she was lost. Not geographically, but within the geography of her own reality, in her own mind. She'd moved with purpose as she came toward him, but the expression in that child's eyes.... He'd seen that look overseas, too. In kids of war and their parents, and occasionally in his fellow soldiers. He wasn't one of those guys who woke in the night with sweats and nightmares. But he felt it in other ways. So, the child had walked toward him and into the road, and he exited the car. The girl delayed him long enough for the woman to come flying out of the house chasing after her.

It hadn't gone exactly as planned, but no harm done. He always focused on getting each day's work done well, doing his duty. That's how he lived his life and did his job and it gave him satisfaction.

He would report back to his client and maybe that would be that. He could put the girl with the lost eyes, and the woman with the wild hair and the most piercing eyes he'd ever seen, behind him, and move on to the next job. He had a few calls to return and with luck the next client would be more interesting and more challenging...more impersonal.

He parked at the hotel, still thinking about it. *Personal.* Was that what was troubling him? The job should never feel personal.

What was different this time? Was it the child? The woman?

It certainly wasn't the client, but that's who was paying the bill.

Greg was ready to move on. Finish this. He dialed the client's cell number. There was no answer so he left a message.

"I found her. She's where you thought. At the beach, that is. Nothing much to tell. I'll give it another day and call you back tomorrow afternoon."

****

Clair

Clair fixed Darcy's lunch. After the meal was done, she brushed her sister's hair with slow, gentle strokes that always relaxed her. She settled her down for a nap. When Darcy rolled over and curled up, Clair relaxed.

She really wasn't made for this job. Would she have been a better caretaker if she were Darcy's mother? Did maternal instincts come to the rescue in cases where the woman wasn't naturally gifted as a caregiver? She loved her little sister, but this hadn't been her life until now and hadn't been planned for.

She reminded herself, yet again, that the loss of Sean and all they'd been building hadn't been planned for either. For a while, creditors had chased after her, hunting for Sean, and if not Sean, then for someone from whom they could recover monies through bank accounts or other assets. Their approach had been increasingly threatening and merciless, especially since she'd lost everything, too, including her hopes and dreams and the man she loved.

Mallory had said, "Thank heavens you weren't married yet. Your name's not on that business or a mortgage." But Clair couldn't make the pivot that easily—going from long-made plans of a future with Sean to being penniless and besieged. Yet she couldn't bite back at Mallory. Mallory had her own heartache and had stepped up to take care of their sister when it counted. She knew, in her head and heart, Mallory was trying to tell her that, along with time and nature, a person had to move forward, one foot in front of the other. You might not get the future you wanted, or thought you wanted, but the future would still arrive each morning and it was up to you to make it worth getting up for.

About six weeks after Sean's abandonment, the creditor calls stopped. Just like that. By then, broke and unemployed, she needed somewhere to go, a fresh start, and she took refuge with her sisters. She and Mallory helped each other and thereby helped Darcy, too, she hoped. Mallory insisted that with time, patience and love they'd all get healed and be themselves again.

Clair had said, "Shouldn't we try another therapist, Mallory? Someone trained to deal with this...withdrawal...."

"We've done that. None of them seem trained for this. They want to try this pill or that therapy, and so on. I won't have her further traumatized by being treated like a guinea pig. For now, let's just give her time."

But Clair wasn't emotionally or professionally equipped to deal with this sort of caretaking either. She wanted a life for herself and Darcy, too, and she didn't see how love alone could make Darcy well. Was that just what you had to believe when you had nothing else to hang on to?

Somehow that thought led her back to the stranger they'd encountered an hour ago. He'd grabbed Darcy's attention for reasons Clair would never know. He had nice eyes. Maybe hazel? Gray? Light-colored eyes, anyway. Attractive face. A little rough looking, but in a nice way, which might not make sense, but that was how she felt about it. A broad jaw, high cheekbones, unusual eyes...in the end, all the usual features that made up a face. Clair decided the sum of his features was intriguing.

What had led him past the house this morning? If he hadn't been there, how far might Darcy have wandered? She was carrying her bucket. Clair shivered.

She needed to speak with Mallory about getting locks installed that Darcy couldn't reach.

After naptime was done, they spent the rest of the afternoon reading (with Darcy staring at the page while Clair read aloud) and working puzzles with little engagement from Darcy. Mallory called and said she was bringing home pizza for supper. Clair said, "Let's go set the table."

Darcy's help was more euphemistic than actual, but she did straighten the napkins that Clair set next to the plates. Clair made a salad, saying aloud, "Pizza, Darcy. Yum, right? We love pizza." And the inane sound of her voice, alone and fake-sounding, proclaiming the wonders of pizza, irritated her. Darcy was restless, too. She went to the front door with her bucket.

"No, it's not beach time. It's suppertime. Mallory will be home any moment."

Darcy went to her room and Clair was relieved. Her brain felt too full. She was as restless as her little sister.

An argument she and Mallory had had a year ago, before that trip to the Caribbean and even before she and Sean had set the date, kept wanting to replay in her head. Clair had said, "We're engaged."

Mallory said, "You only see what you want to see.

You are so stubborn. So blind."

"Blind?" Clair had asked.

"Blind when it comes to what you want. You see everything in those terms. You are the very definition of rose-colored glasses."

"And you are all about reality, but guess what? You see reality through your own eyes and your own opinions. How is that any different, really?"

Mallory flung her arms wide in frustration, then grabbed Clair and hugged her. "I'm sorry. I don't want you to be hurt by him. No more hurt for any of us. Losing mom and dad...this family has had enough."

"Oh, Mallory. I agree. All that's changing now. Our business is going strong and Sean and I are planning our future. I want you and Darcy in the wedding." She expected her sister to cheer with her about the engagement, but her response was far from it. In a softer tone, Clair added, "Next year everything will be different for us. All of us, all good. You'll see."

Ugh. Well, it might not have turned out good, but it certainly was different. Different than she thought it would be.

Mallory could be bossy and occasionally utter an "I told you so" but she never complained despite the responsibilities that had been thrust upon her. Clair admired her and wanted to be that kind of person.

Clair was still waiting for Mallory and pizza when she realized Darcy had been absent for a while and went to find her.

She was in the bedroom—Clair's bedroom—and the closet door was open. A pile of white satin and lace was on the floor and it was moving. Clair rushed forward.

"What are you doing?" It was as if everything, life itself, was conspiring against her. The dream. The bad memories that wouldn't release their hold on her. She'd tucked that gown way back in the closet the last time Darcy had tried to get at it, but it had been a while. Clair thought she had forgotten about it.

Clair reached deep into the folds, trying to untangle her sister who was squirming and making panicky noises. There was a hint of roses in the air. This had been her mother's wedding gown. It didn't fit Mallory, but Clair was built more like their mom and she'd planned to wear it for her wedding. The scent of roses must be permanently embedded in the fabric because when handling the gown, she would often catch a whiff of roses. Despite the passage of years, despite the gown being cleaned, her mother's scent lingered. The scent she'd filled the house with. And now, yet again, Darcy had been in Clair's closet, pulling the garment bag out, and getting the dress free, making a mess and bringing the pain back, keeping the memories sharp and biting. Clair was very close to losing control as she tried to free her sister without damaging the gown. Ugly feelings were trying to form words and were almost said. Mallory arrived before that happened.

"I've got this," Mallory said, stepping into the room and putting her hand gently on Clair's shoulder. "I'll take care of Darcy. Go cool down until we're ready to eat."

Clair went out to the backyard. She sat on the bench and tried to breathe. She touched the blossoms on the azaleas, avoided the thorns on the entwined rose bushes, and whispered, "Mom. Dad. What are we supposed to do? Why did you leave us?" She gulped. "Darcy needs you and so do I. We all do."

****

Clair believed in the power of exercise, sunshine, and a good ocean breeze. Darcy seemed to agree. She was determined again the next morning, walking through the house with her bucket and making small noises. Clair's distress from the evening before was mostly gone, and she was determined to move on emotionally and perhaps make a gesture of apology to her little sister. She couldn't help her sister if she couldn't help herself.

She braided Darcy's hair to keep it from wrapping around her face in the onshore wind. A walk wouldn't hurt anyone and the April weather was fine.

No wedding dream last night. That was a plus. And she felt better overall. More uplifted.

The morning before, that man, the stranger, had somehow snared her attention, even aside from the interest provoked by his encounter with Darcy. He was attractive and well-spoken, and very courteous to Darcy. He picked up the spilled groceries. Clair's emotional response had nothing to do with the man himself, and certainly nothing to do with his gray eyes and broad shoulders. There'd been an underlying roughness in his manner, but gentleness, too, especially when he was dealing with Darcy. He was nothing more than a stranger passing through and had gone on his way. But the chance encounter, and her personal reaction to it, seemed to offer the promise of better days ahead for her, of life still to be lived.

When she told Mallory about the encounter—omitting her personal response, of course—Mallory didn't seem concerned. Her sister's calm rationality reset the guilt meter in Clair's brain. Children did wander off and no harm was done.

Today was a new day, and a better day.

As they walked along the beach, Darcy kept veering toward the ocean. Each time they neared the waves, Clair angled them away, not wanting to get wet, but finally Darcy wouldn't move until Clair allowed her to stay in the wet sand area. Darcy would have her way. Clair pulled the towel out of the backpack and sat in the dry sand nearby.

Darcy stood motionless watching the wavelets run up over her toes, and then Clair noticed a change in her posture. A stiffening, perhaps. Darcy stared at her feet and slowly knelt. She reached for a shell left behind by the receding tide, but stopped short of touching it.

Her sister did occasionally notice shells and pick them up, but this time Darcy stared at the shell as if she'd never seen such an amazing specimen. She moved her fingers near to the shell, first tentatively touching the wet sand around it, then the tiny bubbles that formed at the edges. Finally, she touched the shell itself. It was beige and dark brown, shaped perfectly, and the ridges running from tip to hem were well-defined.

Darcy touched it, pushed at it gently, then picked it up from the sand. She wrapped her fingers tightly around it. She stood. After that she was content to walk again. Clair abandoned the towel on the sand and strolled with her. She wanted Darcy to rinse the sand from the shell, but nothing could persuade her sister to unclench her fingers. She was still clutching the shell when they returned to the path. She refused to put it into the bucket, but stood quietly while Clair helped her step into her sandals.

As they emerged from the path, Darcy stopped again. Clair was puzzled, then saw the dark car. It was the same car they'd seen yesterday. There had to be a million sedans just like it. But she knew immediately, as Darcy apparently did, that the stranger was back. Clair was trying to decide what to do when Darcy moved forward. Clair was forced to follow.

They saw the man, himself, standing in the street a few yards away.

Clair didn't try to hide her suspicion. "What are you doing here?"

He looked surprised and uneasy in that first moment, then he smiled. "I was returning to my hotel." He gestured down the road. "A mile or so that way. On impulse, I stopped here. Thought I might take a walk on the beach."

"The hotel has a nice beach."

"True. But once I'm back there, I'll get sucked into

work and never make it back outside."

She understood how that went. It rang true and she relaxed a bit.

"Was that where you were headed when we saw you yesterday?" She tightened her hold on Darcy's hand, the free hand, not the one holding the shell. She swung their clasped hands a bit, not sure whether she was trying to appear relaxed or ready to move. "You're here on business?"

He nodded.

She motioned toward the path. "It's a lovely morning on the beach. Don't work too hard. Make sure to enjoy yourself while you're here." This was the moment to break off the encounter and stop spouting words that were beginning to sound foolish. He nodded and gave her a quick smile as if he understood and agreed.

But her sister refused to move.

"Come on, Darcy."

Nothing. Clair was about to grab her arm. This time she'd have to be more forceful. But then Darcy held out her hand. Her fist, really. Toward the man. She unlocked her grip and her fingers spread wide revealing the sandy shell in her palm. She held it, offering it. Clair cast a quick, warning look at the man.

He returned Clair's look, uncertain. She nodded yes. But he didn't take the shell from Darcy's hand. Instead, he knelt, extended his own hand palm up, and waited.

Clair tried not to speak. She didn't want to risk disturbing whatever was happening. For a long minute, no one moved, and then Darcy's small hand did. It crossed the inches between her hand and his, and turned over in slow motion to allow the shell to fall gently into his. As it did, Darcy's expression didn't change but the man's polite smile morphed into a glow that lit his whole face and echoed in Clair's heart.

Foolish. Clair heard the word in her head, but she allowed herself a moment to recognize and appreciate the feeling. She hadn't felt this emotional rush since the early days with Sean, back when things had been blissfully good. Their relationship had its ups and downs, especially as the business setbacks worsened, but Clair never doubted the two of them had something good going. She'd trusted in them and their future. It hadn't worked out. Maybe, she'd been foolish to believe in them as a couple no matter what...and maybe she was indulging in foolishness now, but she allowed herself to experience that burst of joy before tamping it down.

"We have to get home." She took Darcy's hand

intending to leave.

"Wait, please," he said. He spoke softly. "Thank you very much, Darcy, for this gift." He stepped away.

Clair felt a bit like a child who'd been let out to play, but too briefly, and was disappointed and resistant, and also like a child who'd been reaching for the flame when someone intervened and snatched her hand back. She was grateful to be saved from near disaster. Of course, she was. She and Darcy started to walk away, yet her own feet felt heavy, almost dragging. Darcy was having the same problem. Clair was afraid Darcy was about to refuse to move altogether when the man called out.

"Wait."

Clair paused and turned back toward him.

"I'm sorry. I just realized I haven't introduced myself. I mean, I won't be here long but we might run into each other again or," he paused as he smiled at Darcy, "in case other gifts may come my way, you should know my name, right?"

"Please." She smirked. His premise was too silly to give credence to. Just plain silly. Darcy, who, to all appearances had been staring at the ground when he smiled at her, was clearly aware of the social interactions happening around her. Clair felt that awareness emanating from her, perhaps like an aura. Or an electrical field. Why? Was it this guy?

"My name is Greg. I'm Greg Prescott, originally from Kansas, but more recently from California."

"California by way of Kansas?" Silly, again.

"Well, not all at once."

Clair glanced down at her sister and then back at the man. What harm could it do? He was just passing through. She said, "I'm Clair. You already know my sister, Darcy."

"Pleased to meet you both, officially."

"Mr. Prescott...Greg, we don't want to hold you up. I'm sure you have business to attend to and it's time for Darcy's lunch."

"Of course."

But when Clair moved, Darcy didn't.

Now what?

He said, "May I walk you home?"

His offer felt like a rescue.

Greg

He could hardly believe he'd introduced himself to the surveillance subject, and then invited himself along for a stroll.

It was the gift. The child had surprised him.

He'd watched the two of them walk along the street this morning and turn down the beach path. The child, swinging the bucket, made their destination obvious. Greg had followed at a discreet distance partway down the path, just far enough to observe them quietly for a few minutes and to verify they weren't meeting anyone, then he returned to the road and shook the sand out of his shoes. He considered returning to the hotel, but he couldn't do the job from there. So, he would wait here. His car was parked beside a low, shady tree with the windows rolled down. When he sat in the car, the paper in his pants pocket crackled. He pulled it out, unfolded it, and took another look.

A photocopy. The name, Clair Bennett, was written in a woman's hand, so probably Clair herself had written it. Below it was an email address that didn't work. Deliberately fake. A faint rectangular outline framed the writing, suggesting the original was a business card. His client, the annoying guy, had given him this and said, "Find her. Don't contact her. I want to know where she is and what she's doing."

The guy had been to the Caribbean. Some fancy resort down there. He said a bottle had washed up at his feet. The client said he had learned to pay attention to the unexpected. Greg understood that.

Greg respected instinct. Not necessarily to blindly follow one's instinct, but to respect it and give it due attention. Maybe that was what his client was doing. Though, to be honest, the guy had irritated him right from the start.

He refolded the paper and returned it to his pocket, then waited and watched. He made sure he was out of the car giving the appearance of coincidentally walking by when the woman and the child emerged from the path. He said hello to them and then, soon after, had introduced himself.

Why? Probably because the child had offered him the shell as if it were the most precious gift ever bestowed.

It had knocked down his defenses—the shell in his hand—given by a child who never spoke. That's what caused him to speak, to offer his name. And why not? Where was the harm? His name couldn't possibly connect him with his client. If Clair Bennett did have some interest in his client, in her mind he, Greg, wasn't part of that lineup. Besides, friendliness could disarm her and he might be better able to assess her current situation and obtain better information for his client.

They exchanged a few courteous words and then

the woman said it was lunchtime. It was a good time to break off the encounter, but the child dragged her feet. Clair looked frustrated.

Impulsively, he said, "May I walk you home?"

Her slight frown cleared and she said, "I guess that depends." She looked down at the child and then back at him. "Maybe just get us started? Maybe she'll keep going. I don't want to interfere with...whatever you were doing. What *are* you doing? You said you were taking a walk?" He saw doubt in her eyes as they fixed on his loafers and slacks. He prepared himself to be challenged, perhaps to be ordered to leave them alone, and that might have been for the best, but then the doubt cleared from her face and, curious, he waited.

Clair

He wasn't wearing a jacket today. She was surprised to realize she remembered his attire from the day before, that she had even noticed it.

She laughed. "You must be a city guy. You're wearing the wrong clothing for the beach. Those shoes will fill up with sand and wreck your socks, too. You need sandals."

He looked down at his shoes and laughed.

"You're right about that. My shorts and sandals are back on the west coast. Not much good to me here. Taking a walk on the street might be a better idea anyway, and helpful, too." He nodded toward Darcy.

Clair hesitated, then said, "I don't know why she's being so stubborn."

They moved together along the street. It was a slow walk, but her sister was heading in the right direction.

"Apologies in advance, but I'll ask anyway because I'm leaving soon and I want to know. Do you mind?"

"It depends on the question."

"This is a beautiful area. Do you live here?"

She shrugged. "I grew up here."

"It must be quiet in the winter."

"It is. That can be nice, too."

"I see. I'm sorry, if that was a hint that I'm talking too much." He waited for the expected response and got it.

Clair said, "Oh, no. That's not what I meant."

"Well, caution would be understandable. After all, we're strangers. It's just that I look at you and I see a mystery."

"Mystery? Nothing mysterious here."

"Now, me, I have no mystery. I was in the service, army, and recently left. Thought I'd enjoy business for a change."

She frowned. "Business? Is that the Kansas or California part?"

"Kansas is where I grew up. California is where I live now."

"Doing business. Yet it brought you here?"

"It did. Not too tough a place to spend a few days."

"I have to agree with that. What kind of business?"

He shrugged. "The kind where people pay you and no one is shooting at you or making you do PT."

"PT? Oh, you mean like working out? Physical training."

"Correct. Don't get me wrong. I like to work out, but I'd rather do it on my own terms, not because I'm told to or have to pass some sort of evaluation."

She smiled. "Sounds like you got tired of being told what to do. But that's true of business, too, isn't it? Maybe not the PT, and while it may sound simple—to be involved in some sort of business—it isn't necessarily. Any business where you have to rely on other people, or on market drivers, or any number of other things...well, as with life, I think control is illusive, or...what do they say? Control is an illusion. Especially if you're partnering with someone." She stopped abruptly.

"Partners. Life is about partnership, right? Even hermits have to work with people from time to time."

She sighed. "This is a strange conversation." In fact, it was crazy. Why was she letting him go on about mystery? He was tempting her to discuss personal matters. Mallory always said she was too open. Why would he care anyway...it didn't make sense...and then she realized he was just making conversation, talking about mystery as an excuse for conversation, almost like a tease...a flirtation. She felt her face grow warm.

"I'm sorry," he said. "I didn't want to invade your privacy. I have to leave soon and I was enjoying the conversation."

He stopped and seemed to be waiting. Clair wanted to shoo him away but the thing was, she was enjoying the conversation, too. When he left, it would be only her and Darcy again. Silence until she chose to fill the air with some inane monologue.

Greg Prescott leveled his gray eyes and high cheekbones at Clair and said, "If I'm being too presumptuous, tell me and I'll back off. Would you consider joining me for dinner this evening?" He shrugged. "I'm leaving tomorrow. It would be nice to have companionship for at least one meal while I'm here."

She was stunned and thoughts were whirling in her head.

In the silence, he added, "Darcy is welcome, too."

Chapter Four

Clair

BEFORE SHE COULD stop herself, Clair said, "My sister can watch her."

He looked a little surprised. She wanted to reach out and pull her words back. There were other words she'd intended to say...words that would keep her safe and her heart—what was left of it—from further destruction. She heard the words again in her head, *my sister can watch her*. She saw how his eyes lit up and how he smiled. And yet....

She added, "Maybe it's not such a good idea. We hardly know each other."

"Somewhere local. A public place. People meet new people every day. I'm safe. I'd tell you if I weren't."

She laughed at the absurdity of that statement and at the twinkle in his eyes. An hour or two at most in a restaurant with a handsome man who seemed to enjoy her company, an adult with whom she could chat and joke—she could do far worse. And he was leaving tomorrow. There was comfort in that, too.

He sensed her trying to decide. "What time can I pick you up?"

She shook her head. "How about PORT OF CALL? It's in Salter Path on the main road. I'll meet you there."

"Sure. Sounds good. What time?"

"Six? Though if my sister has to work late we may need to cancel."

He wrote his phone number on a slip of paper and offered it to her. "Call me if that happens. We'll work something out."

He walked away. She stood there wondering what idiocy she'd agreed to, until Darcy squeezed her hand. That alone was pretty remarkable.

Clair smiled at her, gave hers a gentle squeeze back. "Understood."

After getting Darcy settled with lunch, Clair called Mallory.

"What time do you think you'll be home?"

"Not sure. Why? Do you need me?"

"Well," and then there followed a long pause.

"What? Is something wrong?"

"No, nothing. It's been so long since I went out in the evening, it feels odd."

"Out? As in with friends? Or on a date?"

"Sort of a date, I guess."

"Who?"

"His name is Greg. He's not from around here and he's leaving town soon, so it's harmless."

"Harmless? Clair, really?"

"Really. He was born in Kansas, served in the military, but he lives in California now. He's here on business and he thinks it's okay to wear loafers on the beach. Pretty harmless, I'd say."

Mallory was laughing so hard, she started coughing.

Clair yelled through the phone. "Are you okay?"

"I'm fine. Really. Oh, Clair. You said you just met him? You know a lot about him. Tell me this, though. If he's harmless, then why bother?"

This time, Clair had to choke back a laugh. "Mallory. Seriously."

"You know what I mean. I'm not suggesting you date Jack the Ripper, but someone whose company you'll enjoy...not just a replacement for you-know-who." Her voice softened. "Honestly, I'm glad you're open to getting out again. I think that's a good thing."

"Thanks. What time do you think you'll be home? He mentioned meeting at six p.m. at the restaurant."

"You're meeting him there?"

"My choice. Feels safer. I've had enough drama in my life to last me forever."

"Six. I'll be home by five-thirty. Will that work? I'll try to get home earlier so that you can get dolled up without having to watch Darcy."

"Thanks, Mal. Appreciate it."

"My pleasure, sis."

"I owe you. We need to give some consideration to your social life, too."

They disconnected. Had Mallory really spoken the words "dolled up"?

That thought drove Clair to her closet. She hadn't dressed for a date in a long time. She and Sean had been very casual and worked a lot. Their lives had been like one long date dedicated to their future, the business, plans....

Done. Shut off the negative thoughts. Clair reminded herself that the past was the past. Let it stay there and die there.

This dinner invitation was a date. A real one, but also a test. It was an opportunity to start making new memories to push out the old ones. She and Greg would have a congenial meal together and then he'd leave town. No muss, no fuss. A nice evening out.

She was ready for that.

****

Greg

Should he feel guilty at the deception? No. He would move on and they'd never know anyone had been here investigating anyone. He would be no more than an anecdote, if he was remembered at all. The strange guy who was here for a few days—from California by way of Kansas. Had he really said that? Yes. At the beach access. He shook his head.

Growing up in Kansas seemed a lifetime ago and he'd learned by painful experience that you couldn't always go home again. Home moved on without you. It was how life worked. You expected to pick up where you left off and discovered you didn't fit in any longer. Didn't belong. In fact, it would've been more accurate to say California by way of the Middle East—now just a guy who was passing through Emerald Isle on business. Sand and more sand. At least, California and North Carolina offered boogie boards and oceans with their sand, not to mention a whole host of other conveniences.

As for questioning whether deception was acceptable, or whether the unintended conversation was a mistake...well, personal mission debriefs were a habit and a useful tool. Inviting the surveillance subject to dinner was unusual. That action had been deliberate.

Greg had this odd, yet interesting feeling that he had disclosed more about himself than he'd unearthed about her. He couldn't decide how he felt about that, which itself was illogical.

He put off calling the client. Kilmer was on California time anyway. Meanwhile, he waited near the entrance to the PORT OF CALL. He brushed at his shirt and knocked some sand off his shoes.

Unless he learned something unexpected at dinner, this job was done. Only the wrap-up with the client was required and that would be brief.

He would hit the road in the morning and the next day, he'd catch the flight back to California.

****

Clair

Clair arrived shortly before six. Greg was standing on the sidewalk. He walked forward to meet her as she exited the car.

"I'm glad you came," he said.

"Did you doubt that I would?"

After a pause, he answered, "I wasn't sure. I'm

glad you did, but I wouldn't blame you for having doubts. We only just met. I don't have anyone local to vouch for me."

She smiled. "Darcy approved you, remember?"

"Kids and dogs, right?"

"Absolutely." She was walking on air—that's how light she felt in her sundress and heeled sandals with a sweater over her arm in case it was chilly in the restaurant. Dressed up a little, feeling special, and accompanied by an attractive man—it was a nice change. She checked the state of her broken heart. It was only mildly tender. She took that as a triumph.

He held the restaurant door open for her. "After you?"

They were seated at a table with a view of Bogue Sound. The waitress took their drink orders. The sky was a mix of clear blue and white, puffy clouds. Clair thought Mother Nature might treat them to a lovely sunset. She noticed Greg was leaned back in his chair, relaxed. Funny, it was the first time she'd seen him sitting. Relaxed or not, he cast more than a few looks out the window.

"This area is new to you."

"It is. It's beautiful. The California coast is beautiful, too, but this...seems more peaceful.

More...removed from the rest of the world." He added, mostly under his breath and not really intending to be heard, "I keep forgetting I'm here on business."

"That's how it should be, I think. As for peaceful, this time of year is, but in the summer, all these houses and condos are rented by families and it gets quite hectic. That said, I've seen other east coast beaches in summer and compared to them, the Bogue Banks stays quite calm. It's perfect for families. I've never been to the west coast." She sipped her sweet tea. "You're from Kansas, you said?"

"Long time ago. Not sure why I said that anyway. It would've been more accurate to say California by way of a lot of other places."

"With the military?"

"True."

"You didn't go back to Kansas after your service?"

"They say you can't go home again, right? Home moves on with time, and without you. The geography might still be there, but everything you remember has become part of the past."

Her expression turned solemn. "Sorry. I wasn't trying to make you sad."

"No, it's okay. I know exactly what you mean...not about coming home after military service, but in general.

71

I came home, too, you know. Home. And it is home. But it's different now. I'm different. It's different."

They paused to give their food orders. Greg ordered salmon and she ordered shrimp. "And Sea Biscuits," Clair added. "They're delicious, Greg, and it's been ages since I've been here." As soon as the waitress left, Clair asked, "What do you do now? For a living, I mean."

He took a sip of water to draw out the moment and give himself a second to think. Always best to keep it simple.

"Contracting. Related to industry stuff. Very boring."

She frowned, then smiled. "Meaning you can't discuss it?"

He shrugged, answering her smile with his own.

"No problem. I understand."

"What about you?"

"Me? Nothing. I take care of Darcy. I used to work in business, but...that ended."

Mallory had told her over the years that she, Clair, wore everything on her sleeve like a beacon—her feelings, her history, everything. Mallory said Clair trusted too easily and cared too much. Clair could've sworn that was a thing of the past after what she'd gone through with

Sean, and yet...that old feeling was trying to return. It whispered in her ear. *Why bother hiding? Be yourself. Be who are and you'll attract people who enjoy what you enjoy.*

Clair wanted to welcome the old feelings, to be herself again. She couldn't help wishing the restaurant had music and a dance floor. An excuse to be held close and to decide whether she wanted that to continue. Because she wore her heart and words on her sleeve, she said, "You aren't married, right? I guess I should've asked before."

"No, never have been."

Clair nodded, feeling the warmth of a blush on her cheeks, and glad that he hadn't run in fear. Well, anyway, this whole date, had been his suggestion, so any awkwardness would be his fault, not hers.

She shrugged. "I've learned it doesn't pay to take things for granted. I was engaged a while ago and it ended painfully, so I'm a little...." Mallory was right. Clair knew it. Here she was, about to blurt out the whole sad story.

"Don't apologize," he said. "People are...people. They aren't always reliable or trustworthy. I'm sorry that happened to you."

"You're leaving soon, right?" Suddenly, she felt the need to remind herself of that important fact.

He nodded. "I am. Doesn't mean I won't come back."

"True." But the word sounded small, and suddenly the fear was back, the fear of being hurt and left to pick up the pieces. Some things, like hearts, couldn't be mended, not totally.

Greg leaned forward with his hands on the table. "May I ask something personal? It's not idle curiosity."

"What?"

"Darcy. What's wrong with her? Sorry, that doesn't sound sensitive, but I don't know a better way to say it."

"Our parents were older when she was born." Clair added, "What I mean is Mallory and I were already living elsewhere when they died in a drowning accident about three years ago. Darcy hasn't been the same since. We weren't here when it happened. Mallory returned home to take care of her."

He leaned forward again. "I'm sorry. Was Darcy injured in the accident?"

"No. She was nearby but not actually involved. She was on the beach alone for a long time, waiting...." Clair trembled and broke off, moving on to practicalities. "The doctors ruled out any kind of physical injury. Darcy cut herself off from the rest of the world. She was six, almost seven, and it was as if her life, her…" She searched for words. "Her social growth, her interaction with the world around her, was suspended."

Clair stared at him. "She's in there, and occasionally there will be a connection, like with you. And the beach. She loves the beach. Something will happen…there'll be some tiny change and we start thinking she'll come out of it, be herself again, but no, she goes back into this…state. They call it mutism."

"I've heard of it. Seen it." He looked away. He seemed to be staring at a boat making its way up the sound in the failing light. "It's different for everyone…that breaking point…the last event, the one you can't shake off and walk away from."

She saw empathy in his eyes. "Like on a battlefield?"

"Like that. Yes." He shook his head.

"According to the doctor and therapist, there are different kinds of mutism. For instance, with selective mutism, children go silent or have extreme trouble communicating in certain situations or with specific people, so it's selective as to place, people or time. For Darcy, they ruled that out because she was a little shy, but otherwise fine before the accident. The medical professionals decided it was traumatic mutism caused by losing her parents. They tried different things, therapy and medication and such for a while, but it didn't help. It seemed to drive her deeper into that world. Her world. We're like satellites moving on the periphery."

Clair pressed the corner of her napkin to her eye. She refused to cry. She cleared her throat.

"My older sister Mallory decided to give Darcy time. Time to heal. I worry though. Are we giving her time? Or are we giving up on her? It feels like we should be doing something."

She shook her head. "One of the therapists suggested she was silent because she was seeking attention, or because she was angry. That's when Mallory cut them out. She said Darcy wasn't going to be anyone's guinea pig...but I wonder...." She took a deep breath. "Sometimes I think she's waiting...waiting for our parents to come home." The last words barely made it past that constriction in her chest...the burning eyes. Clair blotted her eyes again and was grateful she'd gone light on the eye makeup. "Sorry."

Greg reached across the table and took her hand. "I'm sorry. I apologize for asking about a private situation and hurting you."

She shook her head, trying to regain her control.

He continued to hold her hand. "You may be

right, though. Maybe that's why she likes the beach so much. That's where she lost them. Maybe that's where she thinks they'll return." He went silent for a few moments, then he added, "So the plan is to love her and care for her and hope that one day she'll be her former self again?"

Clair nodded. "I know that sounds lame, but for now, that's the plan." She nodded, but it was those words he said...*maybe that's where she thinks they'll return to*...that she kept hearing in her ears.

The food was delivered during that conversation, but Clair hardly remembered eating. Their conversation continued as the sun set and night moved in, but it was more general, as if by unspoken consent. Inconsequential chit-chat was better for the digestion anyway. And laughter. Laughter was best of all.

"Dessert menu?" The waitress asked and they both jumped.

Clair spoke first. "I think I should skip dessert. It's later than I realized." In truth, it was fully dark.

"Are you sure?" he asked.

"Yes. For one thing, my sister has work in the morning. She often has to start her day early. Not that she has to wait up for me, of course."

"Of course."

"When do you leave? Tomorrow?"

"Yes. My flight leaves out of Richmond the day after tomorrow, but early, so I'll drive up there in the morning."

"Your business went well, I hope?"

A slow smile crossed his face. "Well enough. Hopefully other opportunities will bring me back here soon."

They paused on the sidewalk, his hand lightly on her elbow. He said, "I think she will."

"She will what? Darcy, you mean?"

He nodded. "Luckily, she isn't suffering from physical injury, so time may be the best cure so long as she keeps in touch with real life." Suddenly, his tone changed. "I hope you don't think I'm criticizing. I'm not a doctor, not a psychiatrist or therapist, but I was a soldier and I saw action, and you never know what will trip a person up. Strong men and women, strong hearts and courage, can hit that point, sometimes out of nowhere, and...well, they call it PTSD. Post-Traumatic Stress Syndrome. That's the feeling I get from Darcy. She's a beautiful child, serene even, but I get the feeling that she's trapped inside and looking for a way out. Sorry, I'm not saying this very well."

"No worries, Greg. I'm not offended. We're all

doing the best we can in this life. It's not always easy. I've had my own heartache and I'm sure you have, too. Darcy and I are lucky. We have each other and our sister, Mallory. We have people who love and care about us."

"That's worth more than you may know."

He walked her to her car. "Any chance you'll meet me for breakfast?"

Crazy. Just plain crazy. "I might."

He grinned. "Where's a good place?"

"MIKE'S? Or rather, it used to be MIKE'S. Now, it's called THE TRADING POST. I hear it's good."

"How early is too early? Nine a.m.?"

Her mouth started to shape the word, yes, but then she realized she was forgetting something important.

"I'm sorry, but I can't. I'll have Darcy to care for in the morning."

"Bring her. Doesn't she like breakfast?"

"Well, yes, but restaurants aren't in her routine, you know? She doesn't do well if we don't stick to the routine."

He looked doubtful.

Clair thought of the shell.

"She seems to like you...I suppose we could try. But if it upsets her or there's any kind of problem, we'll slip out of there. I don't want to attract attention. One day, she'll be... Anyway, understand that if we need to leave, we will."

"Agreed."

He waited until she'd climbed into her car and then went to his own.

Clair settled in and fastened her seat belt. His words, those uncomfortable words, still echoed in her head. *She thinks that's where they'll return.* It wasn't as if the thought hadn't occurred to Clair. It had, but not as fully formed as that bald statement. Not with the impact of hearing it from Greg.

Darcy. The beach. Most people, recognizing where their trauma, their tragedy, had occurred, would avoid any place associated with it. Clair had been grateful that Darcy didn't seem traumatized by the beach.

It nearly broke her heart to think of it. Was Darcy's favorite place, the place she wanted to go every day, bucket in hand, the beach because she was hoping to reclaim what she lost there? Deep inside, did she have hope that her parents would return to the last place she'd seen them?

Mallory was still up when she arrived home. She had forms spread across the coffee table in neat stacks and was assembling info packages of neighborhood comparisons, mortgage estimates and rental histories together for clients. She glanced up as the door opened and asked, "How was it?"

Clair joined her on the sofa. "It was great. Too bad he's leaving tomorrow. Or maybe that's a good thing."

"You tell me. Which?"

"A little of both, I think. He invited Darcy and me to breakfast."

Mallory gave her a look. "Really?"

"Really."

"And you're going?"

"I am."

"Good. I have to say it, though. Being the older sister and all, it's part of my job. Have fun but be careful."

She answered lightly, "It's breakfast at THE TRADING POST. I think we'll be safe."

"I'm talking about your heart and your head."

Clair touched her sister's arm wanting to reassure her. "I'll keep that in mind. It won't matter anyway if he never returns."

Mallory said, "He will."

Her elder sister was smart and in many ways, much cleverer than she was, so Clair let those two simple words, *he will*, settle in. Mallory might be right, but Clair didn't have to figure it out tonight.

"Mal, I have a serious question for you."

"Sure. What's on your mind?"

"Do you think Darcy wants to go to the beach every day because she thinks mom and dad will return there?"

Mallory nodded. "Very possible."

"I never thought of it quite like that. I thought...I don't know...that she didn't make the connection directly since they were...recovered days later. Isn't that a bad thing, almost sick, for us to allow her to go down there, play down there, if that's what she's thinking? Hoping for? Isn't it morbid? Aren't you worried it will keep her hoping and waiting?"

"Hoping and waiting? I suppose that's what we're all doing. Hoping for happiness and waiting to find it. Maybe you're right, Clair. But I see Darcy down at the beach and she seems...comforted. Should we take that away from her? Don't you think she'll give it up herself when she's ready?"

"Do you?"

"I hope so. In the meantime, I can't deprive her of what gives her comfort. To what purpose, anyway? To make her face reality? I think she's already living in, and accepting, as much reality as she can."

Mallory groaned and reached for the paper clips.

"When I figure it out, I'll let you know. You can do the same for me. In the end, hopefully we'll each find what our hearts need."

****

Greg

Greg called his client.

He answered on the third ring. Greg heard noises, voices and general party sounds in the background. A woman was laughing, water may have been splashing, and music was playing, and then it faded away.

"Hold on." More loudly, he called out, "Dee, I'll be right back."

Greg heard a soft sound like a door closing.

"Okay. What's up? What did you find out?"

"Nothing more. I found her, as you hired me to do. She isn't anywhere unexpected. She's at her parents' home in North Carolina. Beyond that, there's nothing to know."

Sean Kilmer responded with silence.

"She lives there with her sisters." Greg almost mentioned that she'd referenced heartache, but a flash of insight hit him and he held it back. "There's nothing else going on."

"How can you be sure?"

"Hard to prove a negative, but there's nothing to indicate she has any interest in you."

Another long silence, then he said, "You spoke with her?"

"I did. Unavoidable."

"I told you specifically not to interact with her. To investigate and keep a low profile. Not to do anything to make her suspicious."

"As I said, it was unavoidable, but it's a good thing it happened because otherwise I don't know how I would've found out anything. There is nothing to find out. Three sisters living in their childhood home trying to recover from the death of their parents." He wanted to ask his client a few pointed questions, so much that it burned in him. Plenty to investigate there, without doubt. Suddenly, he was like a dog with a scent finally sniffing out the fox—Kilmer's real fear. Kilmer's elegant fiancé and her wealthy father. He was sounding less like an affluent businessman and more like a weasel afraid of being caught in a vise. Did he really have anything to fear from Clair? It was hard to imagine a scenario where he might.

"You said you came across that bottle down in the Caribbean, right? Long way from California. Why do you think it means anything? If you tell me more, then I can be more effective."

"It was a coincidence. But I don't believe in coincidence. That card she wrote on? The other side had the name of an attorney. When I saw that, it was a warning I couldn't ignore."

"You know her personally, right?"

"Sure. A woman from the past. They can get vindictive. A lawyer won't do her any good, if that's what she's thinking, but I don't need her messing up my present."

Greg almost laughed. It was as simple and basic as self-interest. This guy, his client, had seen the card, both sides, and gotten spooked. He put sympathy and a touch of warning in his tone.

"I've seen it all and you're right about the potential for vindictiveness. Always good to leave things on good terms. Never can tell what someone who feels betrayed or cheated will do. What lengths they'll go to."

There was a very long silence. Finally, Kilmer said, "Do you think she will...did you see or hear anything to indicate..."

"I told you no, but you can never be sure of anything."

He was done with Sean Kilmer. He'd planted

those last worries deliberately. Probably not his most ethical moment.

Greg would send him a bill and beyond that, as far as he was concerned, this assignment was over.

****

Greg shoved his laptop down into the side of his overnight bag. He was on his way out of the hotel room. He was looking forward to seeing Clair for breakfast, and nearly walked past the folded square of paper on the bureau by the television. The photocopy. With his free hand, he grabbed it and shoved it into his jacket pocket. With a last glance around the room, satisfied, he headed out to meet Clair and Darcy for breakfast.

****

Greg saw Clair was already there, settling in at a corner table and getting Darcy arranged with a coloring book and crayons. The table was already a jumble of menus and wrapped flatware, mixed in with the paraphernalia people with kids always traveled with.

Clair smiled as he approached the table. He was very glad he'd asked and that she'd accepted. Darcy didn't acknowledge his arrival, but he was sure that from behind her long lashes, she saw him. Darcy showed no sign of discomfort when he joined them as far as he could see. Instead, she picked up a red crayon and began coloring a drawing of flower petals. He thought Clair seemed pleased and relaxed. Darcy was in the corner on Clare's side of the table.

"Good morning," he said as he took the chair opposite her. He made a point of speaking directly to Darcy, too. "Nice red flowers. My favorite color."

No response, but there was a tiny pause in her coloring motion. He wouldn't have noticed if he hadn't been hoping to see it. He thought he caught a tiny dimple indent her cheek.

They enjoyed breakfast. Darcy only showed signs of distress when the waitress put a glass of orange juice in front of her. Clair intervened swiftly and the error was corrected. Crisis averted, they moved on to general conversation.

"Too bad you're not flying out of a closer airport."

He grinned. "Had I known I'd want to stay longer, I would've planned it differently."

"Plans." Clair said the word ruefully, shaking her head. "There's a few things in my life I might've planned differently if I'd known what was ahead."

"We're better off not knowing, I think."

"Do you really think so?"

"Sure. There are things we'd never attempt if we knew how hard they'd be or how it would end. Yet even while stuff is going wrong we're learning things, and adding that to who we are and who we're becoming." He sipped his coffee. "Without the unplanned stuff, we'd never have the great moments, the life-changing events, that make life worth the hassle." He gave her a direct look hoping to convey a personal meaning, then glanced at his watch.

Clair said, "I guess it's time for you to get on the road."

"Yes."

"I want you to know how much I've enjoyed this. I'd forgotten there was life outside of how we've been living. I think I've been in bunker mode."

"Because of...present circumstances? Or due to that former heartache you mentioned?"

"Former?"

"I hope so."

"Former," she said, then added, "Both." She smiled and her face seemed clear of shadows. "We went from the loss of our parents to her problem." Clair cut her eyes toward Darcy who appeared to not be paying them any attention. "Meanwhile I was wasting my life with a man I thought cared about me, but who took advantage of me. Not only that, but the time, money and energy he took from me, in many ways were also stolen from my family."

The glow on her face, the passion expressed as she moved her body, her hands, when she spoke, her sparkling eyes, some exotic combination of down-to-earth woman and an open-hearted laughter... He tried to quantify it and couldn't. She was the kind of woman he could fall for, maybe fall in...love with?

It shook him. Attraction, yes. Love? What was that anyway? He had his own history of heartaches. He felt empathy, in sympathy with her, her sister, the damsel in need of rescue kind of thing. Suddenly, he felt a little shaky, but then it passed and he felt assured again. They hardly knew each other. He didn't believe in love at first sight. She might be a romantic, true. After all, she had tossed a bottle with a message in it into the ocean. But that wasn't his style. At any rate, he had a long drive to Richmond ahead of him, voicemails to clear, calls to return and new business arrangements to set up. He could do that from the hotel in Richmond and then fly out the next morning.

"Time to be moving on." And yet, he didn't move.

He was surprised.

"It's been fun. Have a safe trip to Richmond, and back to California. We've enjoyed getting to know you." She extended her hand as if to shake his.

He started to respond. His arm started to move, but then, instead, he stood and crossed the few steps to where she sat. After a brief confusion over her untaken hand, her eyes lit and she, too, left her seat.

"Would a farewell hug be acceptable?" he asked.

She laughed lightly. "Of course," she said and moved into the circle of his arms.

It was a brief embrace. Their first. For one thing, this was at a busy diner where people were eating eggs and bacon, and drinking their coffee or orange juice.

"I liked that," Clair said. And then she flushed bright red. "I mean, not the hug, but what you said. Farewell. Fare thee well, right? Not goodbye." She added softly, "The hug was nice, too."

He nodded. He took a moment to clear his head, to think, before he said, "Darcy, I have to go now. I'm sending you a pretend hug."

The child didn't look up, but with one hand she slid the coloring page across the table with such gusto that it almost took flight. Greg grabbed it before it sailed off.

He felt extraordinarily silly holding the coloring page, a morass of red that passionately obliterated the lines. It felt like a trophy.

Greg walked away wordlessly but with a grin on his face. He paused a few feet from the table.

Clair reached for her purse, but Darcy showed no sign of being ready to leave.

"I've got the tab," he said.

"No, wait. You paid for dinner last night."

"I insist," he said. "If you like, we can talk about it when I come back." He added, feeling almost surprised, "I'll be back."

He knew it sounded like a promise. He wanted to regret it, but couldn't.

He stopped at the register to pay the bill. When he reached the door he took a last glance back and caught her watching him. He grinned, raised his hand, and went to his car.

Clair

Clair wasn't in the least hurry. She wanted this relaxed, warm feeling to linger a while. She wanted to remember the conversation and that farewell hug and his grin as he went out the door. But now that Greg was truly gone, Darcy must've decided the show was over and they could go, too. Since they'd occupied this booth long after the food was gone, and the waitress kept giving them that look, she supposed it really was time. Darcy moved carelessly and several crayons rolled off the table. Clair reached down to pick them up and saw Greg's jacket on the chair next to the one he'd been sitting in.

Through the plate glass windows, she'd already watched him drive away. He hadn't returned so likely he still didn't realize he'd left it. Clair gathered up his jacket along with their belongings. Doing anything with children seemed to involve toting along a truck load of paraphernalia. She and Darcy walked out to her car to go home. Same old home, but she felt like she was on the brink of a future worth dreaming of. As if she was finally waking up.

She took Darcy's hand and held it in both of hers. "There's good things ahead for us, sweetheart. You'll see. We're going to be patient, but we're going to make changes, too. We aren't going to wait for life to find us. Or wait for what can never happen. We can make our own choices and we're going to do exactly that."

****

Darcy brought her bucket to their school session. She held it on her lap while Clair read aloud. When the story was done, Darcy stood and held up the bucket.

"It's rest time, sweetie."

Her sister frowned and held the bucket up again.

"Not today. We'll go over your math this afternoon and then we'll do something special. Let's skip the beach today."

Begin as you mean to go on. Right? Time to try on some new habits.

She caught sight of the computer on the corner table. Perhaps it was time to bring back some old habits, too, like the Romantic Hearts Online Book Club. She had been avoiding them, but her interest was stirring again. How were the other gals doing since the trip to Enchanted Island? It would be fun to post about Greg, the handsome stranger who'd brought some life back to the Bennett sisters.

Clair escorted Darcy to the bedroom and tucked her in for a proper rest. One day, her sister would say, "I'm too old for a nap." Clair looked forward to that day and the progress it would represent. She closed the blinds and left the door cracked open while she brought in the assorted accumulation of stuff from the car and carried it into the kitchen.

She put the travel cups in the dishwasher, emptied this and tossed that, then picked up Greg's jacket. She held the jacket draped over arm and smoothed the fabric. What a joy it had been to catch a glimpse into a brighter future. Of a future that didn't include Sean, or thoughts of Sean. Maybe the bridal gown would stop haunting her dreams.

He said he'd be back. She had his phone number. Too bad she hadn't thought of that at the restaurant, but she could call him now and tell him she had his jacket and would hold onto it for him until he returned. She was reaching for her cell phone when she noticed the white corner, the square of paper, sticking up out of the pocket. It reminded her of the paper she'd seen him holding that first day.

Clair touched the edge of the paper. This man had come into her life so unexpectedly. She remembered how she had wanted him to go away because she was worried about nosy neighbors, but Darcy had trusted him right away.

She hung the jacket on the back of the chair and left the paper in the pocket.

At the kitchen door, she stopped suddenly. Could it be a boarding pass? He might have printed it out at the hotel. Well, he could get another at the airport. Or suppose it was something that he couldn't easily replace? She stared at it for a moment before walking back to the table.

She picked up her phone and dialed his number. He answered immediately.

"Hi, Greg. Thanks for breakfast."

"My pleasure. I appreciate you two joining me."

"Have you realized yet that you left your jacket behind?"

There was a long silence before he said, "No, I guess not. Not really like me."

His voice sounded odd, almost testing, non-committal in tone.

"Do you need it? I'll hang onto it of course, no worries, there, but I see there's a folded paper in your pocket. Maybe a boarding pass or something? I didn't want to pry, but wanted you to know in case it's important."

Again, that long silence, then he said, "No, it's not important. Clair—"

She waited. This conversation felt off.

Greg repeated, "It's nothing important. Stow the jacket out of everyone's way. I'll get it when I return?"

His voice ended the sentence with a question mark. It occurred to her that maybe he was disappointed to realize the jacket tied him to coming back. Maybe he was having second thoughts and was glad to be leaving?

"I can mail it to you, to California, if that helps?" Her voice sounded choked even to her.

"No need. I'll be back. I can get it then."

He seemed to accept her offer, without questioning her motive, but to refuse it in favor of picking the jacket up when he returned, as he'd said, so whatever was troubling him probably had more to do with the traffic than her. Was that relief she felt?

"Soon," he added.

Greg

Greg broke out in a sweat. He felt the prickling on his temples. He reached up and his fingers came away damp.

Guilt? No, not about what he'd done. More about how it would look to her.

He knew what was in his jacket pocket. How could he be so careless?

Well, he knew the answer to that. Distraction = Clair. The note, and shoving it into his pocket as he was leaving the hotel, had been an afterthought. In his mind, the job was complete and the paper was no longer needed, but not smart to leave behind. As to the carelessness of leaving the jacket at the restaurant? Again, distraction. Being focused on Clair and not on business.

She hadn't opened the paper. Would she? In his gut, he didn't believe she'd resist long. He'd used up his good luck with too many close calls overseas and not enough good deeds at home. She would unfold that paper and he'd be the loser. Worse, so would she because seeing the note would inflict damage she didn't deserve, all due to his carelessness and distraction.

Chapter Five

Clair

IN THE END, it was Darcy who made the decision, however unintentionally. Her eyes spied that white corner sticking above the top of the pocket and she touched it, feeling the shape and the point, and then pulled it out. Clair walked into the kitchen as her sister was unfolding the paper. Clair eased it from her sister's hands, not intending to read it, but now it was there, right in front of her face, with that strange block of text in the middle of the big piece of paper.

A photocopy. Her name and that email address.

At first, her brain couldn't make sense of it. The handwritten letters, her name.... Was that her writing? Yes. Then the faint edges of the business card that the information was originally written on came together almost before her eyes and she realized. This was a copy of the information she'd put in the bottle back on Enchanted Island and had tossed into the Caribbean.

Almost in shock, she refolded the paper. She slid

it carefully back into Greg's pocket.

He hadn't mentioned it. Why? He said he was here on business. Her? Was she the business?

Creditors? Were they back and spying on her hoping to find Sean, or to trying to wring money from her one more time?

No. The creditors wouldn't care about this message or the bottle even if they knew of it. This paper indicated he was here for some other reason.

Maybe Greg had found the bottle?

If he had, then why wouldn't he say so? If he hadn't liked what he'd seen when he met her, he could've left quietly. No need for subterfuge. Or for dinner or breakfast. And having this photocopy instead of the original…meant something. What?

Was he working for the person who had found it? Someone who'd given him the photocopy?

She snatched the paper back from the pocket and this time unfolded it roughly, not making any effort to be careful. She checked both sides of the paper for clues. Nothing.

She sat heavily onto the nearest kitchen chair. That glimpse of happiness, of a normal, bright future, evaporated like the dream it was. Dreams weren't meant to be lived. For good or ill, dreams were either a cruel tease or a bundle of regrets and fear.

A cool hand touched her cheek. Darcy. She took her sister's hand and squeezed it gently, reassuringly.

If not for her little sister, she wouldn't have known. Greg—if that was his name, if she could trust anything he said—would've counted on her to respect his privacy. The note would've stayed safely tucked away until his return. He hardly sounded worried. That's how little all of this meant to him.

She pressed her fingers to her temples wanting to stop the pulse pounding there. She had a huge headache in the making. She breathed deeply trying to ease the growing anger and distress, but it drove her and she couldn't settle to anything. Her dark mood communicated itself to Darcy who became sulky. She refused to sit quietly during the pretend math lesson. Instead she kicked her legs and flipped the ends of her hair and hummed tuneless notes. It was extremely unusual behavior for Darcy. She carried her bucket around the house, then put on her shoes and stood at the front door. She repeatedly bumped the plastic bucket against it. But Clair couldn't consider any of it thoughtfully because she was consumed with feelings of betrayal and treachery—the old wounds, still sore, mixed with new raw ones—and nothing else seemed to matter.

Cool reason was beyond her.

She said, "No beach today. I can't handle it, Darcy. Please color or something."

It was well into the afternoon. Darcy had finally settled in front of the TV in Clair's bedroom. Clair had a DVD player hooked up and Darcy could watch her favorite shows over and over. TV wasn't a daily pastime for Darcy, so when it was allowed, she was willing. Her current favorite was an animated movie about a fish and she was fascinated.

Clair needed the respite. She sat in the kitchen with her face in her arms, desperate to think clearly. All she could do was to feel. To hurt. She needed to find the rational bits amid the chaos. Finally, she called Mallory. Her elder sister had a knack of zeroing in on the heart of a matter. But she had to leave a voicemail. To Clair, at that moment, it felt like absolutely everything mattered and she couldn't make sense of any of it.

A car drove up. She crossed the room and looked out the window. Greg's car. She took a deep breath. The TV was still playing. Darcy was occupied for now. Clair stepped out onto the porch as Greg was coming up the steps.

She said, "Why aren't you at the airport?"

"You read the paper."

He didn't say it like a question.

Clair snapped back at him. "Why didn't you tell me the truth?"

"I was hired to find you."

She was almost silenced by his unflinching response, as if there could be honesty in dishonesty.

"Who?"

"The guy who found the bottle and your message."

The photocopy was of the card, so that didn't surprise her. But his manner did. There were so many words tumbling around in her head, so many questions.

"Who are you, really? Is Greg your name? Is lying part of your job? Hurting people to get what you want? Is that how you make your living?" Her tone grew more intense as the words grew harsher. The expression on his face stopped her. She couldn't read it. He was flushed and his jaw had tightened. But it didn't seem like anger. More like pain. Was it her job to deal out pain?

"You should leave."

He didn't respond. In that long moment of silence, Darcy screamed.

Clair turned her back on Greg and raced toward the sound of her sister's cries.

The screams led Clair down the hall, past Darcy's

room to her own. There on the floor was a white puddle. No, not a puddle. A billowing, moving cloud of white satin and somewhere beneath it, Darcy was screaming as she fought it.

Clair fell to her knees and touched her sister through the satin, locating her limbs and her head. It wasn't as simple as lifting the gown off. Darcy was tangled in it. She must have tried to put it on.

With gentle touches and calm noises, Clair gradually worked the fabric away from Darcy's face, then the rest of her body relaxed.

She'd forgotten Greg until Darcy's head was freed. The fear in Darcy's eyes vanished when she saw Greg. She pushed the hair out of her face and smiled. Only one corner of her mouth quirked up, but that counted in as a smile big-time in Darcy's world.

"Hi, Darcy," he said. "Are you okay?"

Clair turned quickly, nearly falling into the jumble of girl and satin. Greg was smiling, too. It was a small smile and there was nothing merry in his eyes. Clair knew the smile was intended to reassure Darcy.

"Hold still, Darcy. Let me get this over your head."

She did and Clair soon had her free. Clair held the gown in her arms. The fabric pooled over her legs and across the wood floor. She wouldn't fuss at Darcy, not in front of Greg. Mr. Prescott, rather.

Clair stood, pulled her sister to her feet, and put the gown back on the hangar. She hooked the hanger over the door. She'd wrestle it back into the garment bag later. For now, she would deal with Mr. Prescott.

He was frowning. "What smells so good? Is that roses?"

Exasperated, Clair said, "I think we're done here, don't you?"

Holding her sister's hand, she walked away into the living room.

He followed. "Are we done? It doesn't feel like that to me. Was that your wedding gown?"

"None of your business. None!" She bit her lower lip, trying to calm herself. It was hard to say what was on her mind in a calm, let's-not-upset-Darcy voice.

"Unless you have more to tell me about how you came by that photocopy and explain who sent you and why, then we are most certainly done. Yes."

At that moment, Mallory's car pulled into the driveway and parked beside Greg's. She got out of the car and stood for a second beside the unfamiliar car. She stared at it briefly, then she moved toward the house. Darcy released Clair's hand. She opened the door that Clair had left unlocked and met Mallory on the porch.

Mallory showed her pleasure at being greeted, if it could be called a greeting, by Darcy. Still, it was something and it was different and even no-nonsense Mallory showed her surprise. Her face lit up, then she caught sight of Greg.

Clair said, "Hi, Mal. Mr. Prescott forgot his jacket and came back for it."

Mallory raised her eyebrows, probably wondering at the "mister" reference.

"I'll go fetch it. You've got Darcy?"

She nodded. "Sure." The puzzled look continued. She turned from Clair to Greg and then back to Clair again. "Everything okay?"

"It's all fine. Just fine."

"You don't sound fine."

"I will as soon as I've said...goodbye to Mr. Prescott." Clair snatched the jacket from the back of the kitchen chair. She wanted to throw it at him. Instead, she walked out the door and across the porch, leaving him to follow.

Greg nodded at Mallory and Darcy and then he left.

Clair didn't want to speak to him in front of an audience, whether of family or neighbors. Whatever fueled her anger—probably adrenalin—seemed to be dropping away. She felt vulnerable. She was failing, her life was a sham, her choices were poor, and she didn't want witnesses.

Greg followed her across the yard and walked in the street beside her.

"My sister says I live in a world of rose-colored glasses." Clair spoke harshly. "My ex-fiancé said I was too positive. Too optimistic. That I worried about all the wrong things." She stopped, shook her head and thrust the jacket at Greg, surprising him with the sudden force of it. "Don't underestimate me. I try to be nice to people. Don't mistake that for me being anyone's door mat."

She walked a few steps farther and then realized she was barefoot on the rough asphalt of the road. She stepped off to the side where soft sand filled the verge.

"I don't," he said. "I don't know about the rose-colored glasses thing. I suspect that's true. I don't see that as weak, though. You seem...normal."

"Please don't try to schmooze me. I haven't been normal in a long time. Not since Sean...not since I fell in love with him. I didn't see him as he really was. I only saw the good traits. The energy, the drive."

"He doesn't deserve you."

Doesn't? Not past tense? He'd almost whispered the words. It told her too much.

No more.

Clair walked away, waving her hand and shouting, "Don't follow me. Go away."

She wanted the beach, to smell the salt air, clear the bad stuff from her head and feel small amid the noise and sheer unimaginable size of the Atlantic. There, at the foot of the ocean, she was too small for her problems to have any importance. They were tiny blips in a life. Minor inconveniences. She'd bounce back from them any time now. Her cheeks stung and she reached up thinking to brush away an insect, but her hand came away wet. No, she wouldn't cry. Not here because Greg Prescott was sticking with her. He was only a few steps back.

When Clair reached the path, he called out, "Wait. I need to speak with you. Things need to be said. Running away doesn't solve anything."

She kept her back to him and her face turned away. Soon he was in step beside her again and the beach was in sight.

"You know who sent me," he said, trying to match his longer stride with hers.

"Why? How did he get that note?"

"You mean the message in the bottle."

"He told you about that? How would he know? You're toying with me. Leave me alone."

"You don't really want to turn your back on the truth, do you?"

Clair knew without doubt she didn't want to relive that time, to discuss Sean in any way, shape or form. Not with anyone, certainly not with Greg. Nearly breathless, Clair stumbled through the drifts of dry sand. Greg stepped quickly ahead and grabbed her arm.

"Please listen. He's my client and I shouldn't be saying anything. Confidentiality and all that. The truth is, he never said why he wanted to know where you were or what you were doing. He expressed vague concerns about whether you might be interested in him and where he was. He sent me to find out and to be discreet about it. I wasn't supposed to speak with you, but well, you know how that happened. If not for Darcy, I would've kept going, reported back to him, and gone on to the next job."

Clair tried to listen, to digest his words. "Why? Why would he care? It doesn't make sense. Unless he wanted to...."

Greg

Greg saw the idea complete in her eyes as a sudden light flared in them. He shook his head, and tried to be kind.

"He didn't want to come back, but something was on his mind."

Could he mention the fiancé and her wealthy family? Normally, confidentiality wasn't negotiable. Was it different this time? He thought it might be. That scared him. He pulled back the words that would tell her about Sean Kilmer's current affluence and his own suspicions.

Moving as if dazed, Clair walked slowly toward the ocean. He reached out to touch her arm again. This wasn't done yet.

"Clair."

She appeared not to hear him. His shoes were a handicap in this sand. He kicked them off.

When she stopped abruptly, he did too, but so close to her that loose strands of hair blew back toward him, almost brushing his face. He reached up. Her hair flew on the wind and snared his fingers, but he refrained from catching them.

"He gave you that copy of my message?"

"Yes."

"How did he get it?" She spun around and shouted at him, repeating, "How did he get the note from the bottle?"

Greg was stunned by her sudden rage and the way her face flushed and her eyes glittered. Her hair was blowing wildly across her face and he resisted the urge to reach across and capture the strands to smooth them back, to soothe her. In that moment, what little client loyalty he had left, shifted and shattered. When he saw her tears, he fought the desire to pull her into his arms, and lost. This was insanity, and it was likewise insane as she punched at his chest saying, "Let me go." She dashed her hands against the tears on her cheeks and said, "I'm not crying."

"You're not crying?"

"No. I cry when I'm angry and I'm so very angry that I can't begin to say how angry I am. But these are tears of anger, not 'hurt' tears."

"Okay. Got it. You have every right to be angry...but not at me."

She shook off his embrace. "Why not? You lied to me."

"Sort of lied. I did it because I had a business arrangement with a client that I had to honor. I've cancelled it. He doesn't know it yet, but he'll find out soon. I was going to tell him in person, but I don't know if I'll wait that long."

"You have his phone number? What is it? Where is he?"

"I thought you were done with him?"

"Apparently, he's not done with me, but he will be. Very soon. As soon as I can get at him, he'll be done."

He touched her arms again, prepared to be pushed away once more, but this time she let his hands remain.

"Try to cool down. I can't help you track a man to do him injury. He isn't worth prison."

She frowned. She bit her lip. "First off, don't tell me to cool down. You don't have that right. Second, what I do or don't do, isn't your business either, but no, he isn't worth prison or the damage to my conscience." She seemed to consider and then, more composed, she said, "Fine. I'll hire you. Why does he want to know where I am and whatever else information he was after? I'll pay you and you can tell me what you know."

"I..." he stammered, finally settling for, "I think that would be a conflict of interest."

"Why? Were you saying empty words? Maybe you're still trying to mislead me."

"I wasn't trying to mislead you before and not now." He took her hand and tugged her along with him to the ocean's edge.

"What are you doing?" she asked.

"Breathing. We are going to breathe. Just breathe."

"Breathe? Are you crazy?"

He pointed ahead of them, to the east. "See that horizon?"

She nodded. "Of course."

"Focus on it. Stare at it. You're allowed to blink," he added. "Then just breathe. Let's breathe for sixty seconds...and then I'll do anything you want me to."

Clair

She looked at him, then turned to fix her eyes on that line where sky met ocean. She felt drained. Drained of hope and fight. Empty. Too tired even to reclaim her hand from his. As she breathed, she felt something change inside her. A warm, yet calm feeling began at the top of her head. She felt it grow through her cheeks, her jaw, and then down through her heart and lungs.

"Open your eyes," he said softly.

She hadn't realized she'd closed them. How long had they been standing here? She opened them now, slowly, and drew in a deep breath. She whispered, but loud enough to be heard over the waves, "Now what?"

"Now you tell me what you want."

His voice was calm and steady. She didn't want to break this moment, this spot of clarity and peace, and yet, from within the peaceful center, she saw most of it, everything that made up the chaos, was unimportant. Did she want Sean back? Not in a million years. Did she care what he was doing these days? No. Did she want revenge? What would that cost her? Hadn't she already paid enough for the mistake of loving and trusting Sean?

It isn't even about forgiveness. It's simply about moving on with her life.

She didn't want her life to be held hostage, not to mistakes or regrets, and not by Sean Kilmer. He didn't want her. She didn't want him. Enough.

"Tell me what you want," Greg repeated.

"Nothing. Everything. I want to enjoy my life again."

"You don't need your ex for that."

"Definitely not." Tension threatened to rise again, but she pushed it away and continued staring at the horizon, wanting Greg to speak again yet afraid that he would.

Clair said, "I thought we were working together, building a life and future together. One day it was all good and we were making wedding plans and then suddenly we weren't. He was gone. I couldn't ask questions or ask for a second chance to make it work."

"Do you want a second chance?"

"No. If he could leave me, abandon me like that once, he would do it again." She closed her eyes, then opened them again to focus on that distant line. "I would've skipped that Caribbean trip. He encouraged me to go. He wanted me to scout it out so we could go back on our honeymoon. The two of us were starting the rest of our lives together. It was so romantic. He said he was going to make reservations and...." She squeezed his hand and he returned the gesture. "I guess I did such a good sales job that he went there after all and that's where he found the bottle?"

"A place called Enchanted Island. Yes, that's where he found the bottle."

"He was there with someone else?"

"I believe so."

"If not for the bottle and message, would he have ever bothered to check on me? To find out if I was doing okay? No, wait. He didn't want you to make contact, right? So he wasn't worried about my state or status. He didn't care, even belatedly, how I was doing."

"I believe he was worried you might show up and complicate his new life."

The pain was there, but not sharp. She hadn't realized how the hurt had become so familiar, like a companion. Almost a friend.

"His new life? He has a new one? I shouldn't be surprised. Sean is the kind who'll always land on his feet regardless of who he steps on."

"He's engaged."

Clair felt pity. Not for herself, but for that other woman. "Does she understand who he is?"

"Probably not, but he's more worried about her father than her. He's the one with the money, and he'll want to keep his daughter happy. The last thing your ex needs it to disillusion either of them. That's my guess.

She was ready to nod when she heard a woman's voice calling her name. She dropped Greg's hand and waved.

Mallory was following Darcy who was moving toward them at a determined pace.

"She was upset. I couldn't get her to stay inside. Sorry. It was all I could do to keep up with her. I haven't seen her move this fast since...well, you know. Before."

Her young sister took Clair's hand briefly, then her fingers slipped away. She ran toward the water, then back, teasing the waves, as if this had been her only reason for coming, and yet it was different. Different behaviors.

This was important. This was exactly what was important.

Then Darcy stopped, looking up, perhaps sensing they were watching, and she smiled.

It was short and it was brief but the smile was as real as Clair's best day ever, her best moment, perhaps more so. Clair watched and the smile was repeated, small but deliberate.

"Did you see that?" Mallory asked.

Clair nodded. "She smiled. On purpose. Then she did it again."

Mallory threw her arms around Clair, totally ignoring Greg standing there, staring at them.

Mallory stepped back, laughing. Clair was shocked to realize how long it had been since she'd heard her older sister laugh. Perhaps as long ago as when her younger sister had laughed? They were all damaged. Mallory stopped only to kick off her shoes and then, suit and all, ran to Darcy and took her hand. Together, they played tag with the ocean.

Mallory splashed into the edge of the water, gave Darcy a bear hug, lifting her off the ground by a few inches, then set her back down. Darcy hugged her back. A small hug, but a hug. Clair felt forgotten, but in a good rose-colored glasses kind of way.

Clair touched her forehead, confused or bemused. She wasn't sure.

"Are you okay?"

Somehow Greg's arm had come around her as they stood side by side. She was okay with it. Felt steadied by it.

"I'm fine. Merely...amazed. Signs of progress," she said. "Don't misunderstand. I'm happy about it and I want to let everything else go...but it doesn't seem enough. Sean, I mean. Feels unfinished." She eased away from his arm.

Greg nodded. "Do you really think talking to him will help?"

She went silent. There was no answer to that. She knew Sean. He would either dismiss her, hurting her more, or make her feel ridiculous, or... she couldn't think of any way in which a confrontation would solve anything. It would more than likely feed his ego.

She whispered, "There has to be some way, Greg. Something...."

"Clair."

She looked at him. He was holding a pen.

"Write it, Clair. Write it on paper. Tell him what you most want to tell him." He handed her the ink pen. "Do it tonight. When I come back tomorrow, you can tell me what you want to do with it. I'll take it back to him if that's what you want." He shook his head and made a small noise. "I'll make him eat it, words and paper, if that's what you want."

He could do it, too. She heard the undertone in Greg's voice and she stared at the ink pen.

"Will you do it?" he asked.

She nodded. "I think so." She put the pen in her pocket. The breeze caught her, a cool wind, and she shivered. Mallory and Darcy had traveled a few yards further down the wet sand. They were picking up bits and pieces of tidal leavings.

Sea glass from broken hearts? She shivered again.

"I'll walk you back to the house."

"Was I stupid, Greg? About Sean? About...everything?"

"Stupid? No. You loved and trusted him. He betrayed that. Maybe that's who he is or will ever be, or maybe one day he'll become who he should be, but that's on him. You're done with him."

"I am. But I fooled myself into believing what I wanted to believe. How will I ever trust my instincts, my judgement, again?"

"I don't know. But I'd like to tell you what I'm grateful for. Something a smart beautiful woman did that may well have changed more than one life for the better. Time will tell."

"What's that?"

"I'm grateful you put a note in a bottle with your name on it." He took her hand and placed a gentle kiss in her palm. "Because when you threw that bottle into the Caribbean, the current, in a roundabout way, brought me to you."

"The whole idea was silly. I was just going along with the others."

He continued as if he hadn't heard her. "One day, I'd like to stand in that same spot on the beach, and see where your new life began before you ever knew you needed a fresh start."

****

Clair and Greg walked up the path together following Mallory and Darcy. Clair watched her elder sister and her younger sister leading the way and noticed both gals were carrying their shoes.

No red bucket.

It hit Clair almost like a sucker-punch. Darcy hadn't brought her bucket. *No bucket.* She was carrying her own shoes, like Mallory.

Clair felt the sob rising from within. Mal and Darcy kept going, not looking back, but Greg was there.

He held her while she cried against his shirt. He didn't ask. He didn't advise. He waited until she was done, and then they moved forward again.

At the house, Mallory called out the door, inviting Greg to stay for supper.

"You're welcome to join us."

Greg gave Clair a long stare and then replied, "Thanks. I'm looking forward to getting to know you, but not tonight, I think."

Mallory nodded and went back in the house. Clair waited outside as Greg drove away.

Such a short time since they'd met and so much had changed. Perhaps the Bennett family been on the cusp of change anyway. Was Greg the spark?

****

After supper, Mallory went to the shower to wash off the sand and salt. Clair and Darcy settled at the cleared kitchen table. Clair held a blank piece of paper. Crumpled papers were already scattered nearby on the table, and Darcy watched her, her gaze still somewhat askance, but not hiding her interest. Her coloring book and crayons lay unused beneath her slim fingers, as if waiting.

"Am I being silly? Should I write this letter?" Clair asked her.

She wasn't expecting an answer, and she didn't get one, but Darcy did meet her eyes before turning away and picking up a crayon.

Clair smiled. "It's okay, little sis. I'll figure this out one way or the other."

She dropped the pen on the table, intending to push it all aside. Then, she reconsidered. Levity was called for. To be silly, she picked up a purple crayon and drew an oval then added eyes and a huge nose and a gap-toothed grin. She smiled at Darcy and held it up. "What do you think? Will Sean get the message if I send him this?" Clair laughed. In a softer, regretful voice, she added, "Maybe he'll come home begging me to forgive him, saying he's sorry he left me all alone without even a goodbye."

Darcy's lower lip shook, then she clamped it between her teeth. This was new. The frown that pushed her eyebrows closer together and deepened that line between them, wasn't new. Then her eyes filled with tears—and that was new. Clair put her hand to her forehead as if to still the emotion growing inside her. Almost dizzy with joy, Clair dropped the paper and crayon and dashed around the table to put her arms around Darcy. The child turned her face toward Clair's. The tears on Darcy's cheek wet her own. Clair watched her sister, surprised, but Darcy pressed her face close again. Clair stopped breathing when Darcy whispered in her ear, "Tell mommy to come home."

Clair picked her up heedless of Darcy's height. She hugged her and spun around, and then overwhelmed, Clair knelt, taking them both to the floor. She pressed her hands to Darcy's cheeks and stared directly into her sister's blue eyes.

"You know mommy and daddy would come home if they could? They can't. They don't want you to wait for them. Not for daddy or mommy. They want you to grow up and be a happy girl. Mommy wants to look down from heaven and see you growing and laughing. Do you understand that?"

"Mommy," she said again.

Around them, Clair caught the scent of roses, but not with her nose. She perceived their perfume in her brain and in her heart.

"I would bring her back to you, if I could. I can't. She can't return to us. But you have me and Mallory. We are sisters. You will always have us, Darcy."

Darcy burrowed her face into the crook of Clair's arm and Clair held her tightly. She rocked her while

Darcy cried quietly. As she cried, Clair remembered where she had last smelled roses, where she'd most often caught that scent in the past year—and understood there was no way she could grant Darcy's deepest wish, her heart's desire, but there was a small gesture she could make. An easy gesture that might mean far more to Darcy than to her.

When Clair sensed the storm was passing, she touched her sister's hair, caressing and soothing her, and spoke. "Darcy, I need your help. Can you help me?"

Her sister looked up, her face streaked, and she nodded. Direct interaction again. Clair wanted to cry, too, but was afraid Darcy would misunderstand. Her voice sounded rough as she said, "Thanks so much. Come with me and I'll show you what I need your help with."

They held hands as they walked to Clair's room. There was strength in Darcy's hand, not the usual flaccid grip. When they entered the room, they stopped in front of the closet and Clair opened the door.

"The wedding dress, Darcy. Can you take it from my closet?"

At first, Darcy shook her head. This was a no-no. She always got fussed at for this very thing. Clair said, "It was different when you took it without permission. This time I'm asking you to take it from the closet."

Hesitantly, Darcy stepped toward the hanging clothing. She located the garment bag at the back where Clair had stashed it the last time. After another quick glance Clair's way, and a reassuring nod, Darcy reached up. Standing on her toes and stretching her arms, she was able to lift the crook of the hanger high enough to clear the bar.

Darcy turned back to Clair. The bulk of the garment bag and gown bunched up on the floor. She tried to hold the garment back up high, as high as she could, carrying it toward her sister.

"No, sweetheart," Clair said. "The wedding gown is yours now. Remember that I was going to wear it at my wedding? Well, now I'm not. This gown—this wedding gown—was our mother's. Now, I'm giving it to you. It will be in your care until the day you marry. You'll wear mommy's wedding gown, if that's what you'd like. But to do that you'll have to grow up first and learn lots of things. I will help you and Mallory will help you, but we need your help, too, to make it happen the way it should."

Darcy unzipped a few inches of the bag and reached in to touch the gown and pressed her face close to it. She was surely inhaling that last lingering fragrance of roses. The last tears on her cheek transferred to the gown leaving a splotch of wet.

It had never occurred to Clair before—not so that she'd truly understood—what that gown meant to her little sister, and why.

"It's your job to take care of it now, okay?"

Darcy nodded. Using both arms, she carried it carefully to her room. Clair cleared space at the end of Darcy's closet rod and her sister stretched on tippy toes to hook the hanger over the bar.

From behind them, Mallory said, "It's looks perfect there, don't you think?"

In a voice they hadn't heard for a long time, a voice that had been only a whisper a few minutes before, Darcy answered, "Yes."

"You're welcome," Clair said.

She smiled shyly.

"Darcy, I'm going to finish that note now. I think I know exactly what to say to Sean Kilmer."

Mallory didn't know about Greg's suggestion. She showed surprise, but moved aside to allow Clair past.

Clair paused in the doorway with Mallory. She was almost afraid to leave, that the moment would be gone, perhaps not to return. But the timing was right. She stood with Mallory and they watched Darcy carefully close the closet door, pat the wood and then rest her cheek against it.

****

Greg

Greg waited on the beach near the path. Clair had called to say that Mallory was taking Darcy for an outing and as soon as they were gone, she would meet him there. It wasn't long before she emerged from the path onto the beach. The onshore breeze was gentle. It tossed her hair, including the curls that had escaped from the band she used to try to control it. The breeze tossed the curls and played with the skirt of the dress she wore. Her feet were bare and he could've sworn he smelled roses.

When she reached him, he reminded himself to breathe so he could ask, "Did you figure out what you want to do?"

She held up a piece of paper. It was folded like the sheet he'd carried in his pocket. Like the photocopy Sean Kilmer had given him.

Disappointed or not, he meant what he'd already told her, and he repeated it. "I'll take it to him. I'll deliver it into his hands myself."

"This?" She waved the paper. "No. This isn't for Sean."

He was caught by the expression on her face. He searched, but could find no anger or resentment in her eyes. In fact, there was a difference, perhaps a lilt in the set of her lips. A teasing....

"I tried to write to him, as you suggested. It made sense. But each time I put that pen to the paper, I went blank." She shook her head. "I'm sure if he was here in front of me, I'd find plenty of things to say...angry words, hate-filled words, maybe words that would make me feel pathetic...but nothing that would uplift me. Nothing I could walk away from afterward and say I was better off than I was before all that venting."

He accepted the paper from her. It was folded in quarters, exactly like the paper the client, his former client, had given him.

Clair continued, "Instead, I realized a couple of things. First, I understand now how much Darcy and I have in common."

He shrugged. "You're sisters...."

"In how we handled our losses. Darcy couldn't let mom and dad go. She might find comfort in being at the beach where she spent so much time with them...but that's where they left her. I can almost hear my mom calling to dad, "Help!" and dad saying to Darcy—she was only six—wait here. Don't leave the beach. I'll be right back."

He could imagine the scene playing out in exactly

that way.

"She did as she was told. And me? It wasn't that I wanted Sean back, but I kept replaying it, reliving it. I wanted to understand, as if that would make it right, or at least it would make sense. I wouldn't keep questioning and second-guessing. Then, I realized, Sean didn't have the power to release me. Only I could do that." She stood taller. "I'm doing that."

Her stance, the set of her shoulders and her strong, sure voice grabbed his heart. He never used to be impulsive, but this time he couldn't help himself. He put his hands on her arms and pulled her forward into his embrace. How would she respond? His lips touched hers gently.

She almost kissed him back. Her arms made it up and over his shoulders. Her fingers pressed into his hair, his neck, and her lips met his...but then she stopped. He stared into her eyes, the question unspoken. She stayed in his embrace, but broke away from his gaze as she ran her finger along the side of his face tracing his temple, his cheekbone, his chin, his lips, with her eyes memorizing each line and curve of his face.

He shivered. With a shock, he realized he felt found.

Found. Seen.

How had he never felt that before? He didn't know he hadn't, or that it was something he could feel, until now that he...that he'd been found and accepted.

It wasn't Kansas or California, or any of the stops between. But it might be home.

This time, she pressed her lips to his and within that kiss, along with the salt air and a world of scents borne onshore by the Atlantic Ocean, he believed he was tasting a promise of forever.

Clair

Wasn't he almost a stranger? She hadn't known he was out there living his life, moving about the world the same as she was, and he hadn't known about her. Yet she felt like destiny's fingers were at work here, bringing them together.

If that were true, then instead of blaming anyone or anything for what had happened with Sean, she owed gratitude to a number of people, including her little sister.

Rose-colored glasses? Maybe Clair wore them sometimes. A romantic? Yes, definitely. How else could she believe in love *almost* at first sight?

What was it that Greg had said? About being

grateful to that beautiful woman who'd put these last few days into play by tossing a bottle into the turquoise waters of the Caribbean almost a year ago?

When the kiss was done, done at least for the moment, Clair said, "It started on Enchanted Island." She touched her hand to his cheek. "Everything was going wrong and I didn't know it, not until after I returned home."

Inadvertently, she'd begun fixing the unknown, impending heartache while on Enchanted Island by putting that message in the bottle. If not for that, if not for the bottle washing up for Sean to find, he wouldn't have hired Greg. He wouldn't have sent Greg to her. She laughed.

"I'm glad you're happy, but what's so funny?"

"If I were to send Sean any message at all, it should be a thank you note." She smiled. "But I won't." She touched the folded paper Greg was still holding. She took it from him, unfolded it and held it for him to see.

"It's blank?" he said.

"You bet. This message is for you and I prefer to deliver it in person."

Clair slid her arms around him, and she kissed him again.

Chapter Six

June ~ At Emerald Isle, NC

ONE COULD NEVER know the truth of a person's heart or the secrets they might hide. If those secrets were revealed, exposed to the light of day, most folks would wonder why the person had ever bothered to go to the effort of hiding them in the first place. Daylight often steals a secret's power. The same with fear and hurt. Their dark power wilts when faced and dealt with.

Clair wondered what secrets and fears were on Sean's mind when he sent the check that arrived in May? It repaid that undocumented loan with interest. It didn't cover all her losses from their time together, but it fixed an awful lot of the remaining hurt. She hadn't had to say the ugly words, and Sean had voluntarily made good, perhaps showing she hadn't been totally wrong about who she thought he was when they were together.

Mallory scoffed. She said, "You are truly a romantic. More likely, he couldn't shake the fear that you might show up and contest his rights to that patent."

"You know I wouldn't have a ghost of a chance of winning that."

"True, but investors don't like uncertainty or the dirty laundry that creates it. I think Sean is gambling that you'll take the money and leave him to pursue his new life with Mr. Woodhurst and his darling daughter."

Clair said, "You're probably right. Either way, I'm cashing the check before he has a chance to back out on me again."

One thing Mallory was right about. Clair was a romantic at heart, through and through.

She said it aloud for all the world to hear. She had fallen in love with a man, a stranger for all intents and purposes, somewhere between day one and day three. And, luckily, Greg, no longer a stranger, had returned the favor.

Clair intended to live in the sunlight and sleep soundly at night, even if her older sister scolded her for wearing her heart on her sleeve and making silly, rash decisions. It was far better to share one's heart and risk breakage than to hide it in that dark place along with all those pesky secrets and fears.

They discovered Greg was a romantic, too. Over the course of April and May, he courted Clair with dinners and small gifts and flowers. A silly waste of money, of course. But silliness had an important place in romance and love. If lovers couldn't embrace life and love, then what was the point?

More importantly, Greg also went immediately to work making arrangements to move his life, including his business, to Emerald Isle.

On June 1st, Greg proposed. On the beach, of course—at Emerald Isle, not at Enchanted Island. The waters weren't turquoise but the sun was golden and the sea birds flew by serenading them with their calls as he knelt before her. Yes, he knelt. He took her hand, kissed it, and asked her to marry him.

Her heart glowed so warmly that it lit her whole being.

The breeze blew her unruly curls into her eyes. She brushed them back and said, "What?"

He kept her hand clasped in his. He frowned a little, a pretend frown, and raised his voice to be heard better over the ocean. "I asked you to marry me."

"I know." Clair sank to her knees on the sand beside him. "I wanted to hear you say it again."

"Marry me, Clair."

"Yes," she said, as she kissed his hand and then moved on to his lips.

Epilogue

A Beach Wedding

THEY WANTED A beach wedding. Not at Enchanted Island, in part because Clair wasn't risking any "enchanted" complications. But mostly because Emerald Isle was home. When Greg asked where she'd like to go for the honeymoon, she told him the mountains.

"Rent us a romantic cabin in the Smokey Mountains," she said. "Our destination wedding will be here at home and our honeymoon will be within driving distance." She smiled, her dark eyes fastened on his gray ones. "We'll create our own adventure."

Mallory expressed her concern at the short timeline. It was her job to do that as the big sister, but once done, she hugged Clair and they set to work making the arrangements.

"I wish we had more time to plan."

Clair said, "Keep it simple. This is about love and our future. We have everything we need for that."

"But it's happening too fast."

"I planned before and look how it ended up. I can't say it's smarter to do it this way, but I'm going to give it a try and trust to love."

"I'm a little jealous, you know," Mallory said. "It's so impetuous. But I'm also afraid for you."

Clair kissed her sister's cheek. "Don't be. I've always been a little envious of you, too. Of how you make everything seem reasonable and rational. I want you to know that. But mostly, I want you to know we're not leaving you in a lurch. You will have your own life, too, I promise. Darcy is making real progress, but she has a lot of ground to make up. With the three of us to help and encourage her, she'll come all the way back to us. Her future will be the brightest of all."

The night before the wedding, Mallory threw a magnificent bridesmaids party. The guest list was exclusive. The three sisters ordered in pizza and spent the evening painting each other's fingernails and toenails. Darcy had chosen the color. Red. Simple, solid red, without the white base in Clair's dream. It was a blast. No matter how they reassured her, Darcy spent an hour flapping her hands and blowing on her nails to make sure they dried thoroughly and didn't get mussed.

Darcy still didn't talk a lot—only when she felt strongly about something—yet the direct interaction, the voluntary hugs and smiles, were frequent. Clair caught Darcy trying to read on her own, and she had finally refused to nap, declaring she wasn't a baby. Clair was delighted.

Two weeks after the proposal, Mallory stood beside Clair as her maid of honor, with the additional honor of escorting the bride to give her away. Darcy walked ahead of them, carrying her red bucket, but that was okay because it was filled to overflowing with rose petals. She dropped them as she walked. They scattered on the sand and were picked up by the breeze and set to dancing across the beachfront. The fragrance of roses swirled all around them as Clair walked toward the ocean where Greg stood with the pastor, waiting.

At Darcy's insistence, Clair wore their mother's gown. The white satin and lace was as brilliant as ever. The sisters were barefoot, but the red polish on their nails glistened and the sun cast a gentle glow around them. Clair looked at Greg. Her vision sparkled, not with tears, but with happiness. As he smiled in welcome, Clair noticed that the sky was clear—a perfect, infinite blue with no chance of rain.

THE END

ABOUT THE AUTHOR

Grace Greene is an award-winning and *USA Today* bestselling author of women's fiction and contemporary romance set in her native Virginia (*Kincaid's Hope, Cub Creek, The Happiness In Between, The Memory of Butterflies*) and the breezy beaches of Emerald Isle, North Carolina (*Beach Rental, Beach Winds, Beach Walk, Beach Christmas*). Her debut novel, *Beach Rental*, and the sequel, *Beach Winds*, are both Top Picks by *RT Book Reviews* magazine. For more about the author and her books, visit www.gracegreene.com or connect with her on Twitter @Grace_Greene and on Facebook at www.facebook.com/GraceGreeneBooks.

THE BEACH BRIDES THANK YOU

Thanks for reading Clair's story!

Jenny's book is next.

You'll find a Sneak Peek in the Excerpt.

Meet all of the Beach Brides!

MEG (Julie Jarnagin)

TARA (Ginny Baird)

NINA (Stacey Joy Netzel)

CLAIR (Grace Greene)

JENNY (Melissa McClone)

LISA (Denise Devine)

HOPE (Aileen Fish)

KIM (Magdalena Scott)

ROSE (Shanna Hatfield)

LILY (Ciara Knight)

FAITH (Helen Scott Taylor)

AMY (Raine English)

Turn the page for the Prologue and Chapter One
Excerpt from:

JENNY

Beach Brides Series
by Melissa McClone

Copyright © 2017 Melissa McClone

Prologue

Jenny's Message in a Bottle

Dear Bottle Finder:

You have precisely forty-two minutes to complete your mission or life as you know it will end. If you happen to be color blind and can't tell the red wire from the others, just crack open a beer or unwrap a candy bar and enjoy the next forty-one minutes before it's all over.

Oh, wait.

Wrong mission.

Let's try this again...

I'm on a Caribbean vacation with my girlfriends, and we're tossing messages in bottles into the sea in hopes of finding true love. Please understand that alcohol was free flowing when we decided to do this. No, fruity rum drinks with paper umbrellas aren't really an excuse, but they were delicious! And who knows? Maybe dream heroes do exist and ours are out there!

I'd love to say I'm a complete romantic, and that I believe in my heart of hearts whoever's reading this is my soul mate, but I also think we're one EMP away from an ELE. If those acronyms have you heading to Google to do a search, then you likely aren't my other half.

If by some miracle, or alien intervention, you are reading this and think, hey, this could be the woman of my dreams, then your mission is to email me at the address below if you:

- Are single and male.
- Think something strange did happen in Roswell.
- Know your name will never be on the FBI's Most-Wanted List.
- Aren't allergic to cats or dogs.
- Prefer armchair traveling to jet-setting.

Or... if you're certain I'm not the one for you, but want to let me know where you found the bottle and that you read this message, feel free to email me, too, so I can die of embarrassment.

Cheers,
JH
8675309@...

CHAPTER ONE

Thirteen months later...

AT TWO O'CLOCK in the morning, Jenny Hanford still sat at her desk in the half-lit study on the first floor of her house. Day or night, nothing much happened in Berry Lake, Washington, a small town located north of the Columbia River Gorge. Maybe that was why she'd grown up devouring novels and now wrote books full of intrigue, espionage, and non-stop action.

Jenny stifled a yawn.

Yes, she was tired, but sleep could wait until she finished the draft of her new novel, *Assassin Fever*—the next volume in her best-selling thriller series featuring spy extraordinaire Ashton Thorpe.

Almost there...

As sights, sounds, and smells swirled through her mind, her fingers flew over the keyboard. The tapping sound became nothing more than white noise. She focused on the screen. Letters turned into words that became sentences and then paragraphs.

Her breath caught in her throat.

Tears stung her eyes.

Oh, Ash. You did it. You saved the world. Again.

With a sigh, she typed her two favorite words in

the English language—*The End*. The draft was finished.

Satisfaction flowed through her.

A good feeling considering she'd been certain the story was the worst thing she'd ever written only four days ago. Still not perfect, but the manuscript didn't suck as badly as she'd thought. All she needed was feedback from her editor so she could do revisions. She typed a quick email, attached the file, and then hit send.

Now she could sleep. Well, once her brain slowed down.

If she went to bed now, she'd lay awake. The story still looped through her mind. The elation of finishing mixed with the sadness of saying goodbye for now to her favorite character.

Might as well do something productive until she could sleep.

The number of emails in her inbox made her do a double take. Jenny groaned. She'd been ignoring everything for almost two weeks, but...

8132.

She groaned again.

Don't look at them.

But, of course, she had to.

Jenny deleted as much of the junk as she could. Message notifications from her online book club could wait until tomorrow. They were used to her disappearing to write. When she'd first joined the Romantic Hearts Book Club, she'd been a full-time textbook editor and part-time author. Now she only edited an occasional textbook project—usually as a favor to her former boss—and wrote full time.

So much had changed over the past four years. Her entire life really, though few knew because she'd never made a big deal over writing as Jenna Ford. She wasn't *that* secretive about her pseudonym, but she'd quickly learned too many people only wanted to be *Jenna's* friend. Not Jenny's.

Maybe that was why her closest friends, other than her sister-in-law, were people she'd met virtually. She could just be herself with them. It was easier that way.

She scrolled through her inbox and deleted what she could. The subject line "*Message in Bottle Found*" caught her attention.

She did a double take. "Seriously?"

Over a year ago—thirteen months to be exact—she'd taken a Caribbean vacation on Enchanted Island with eleven other members of her book club. Meeting in person seemed appropriate after being together online for three years.

Boy, was it ever!

Spending face-to-face time with friends, having fun in the sun, and talking about books was exactly what she'd needed. Jenny hadn't realized how badly she'd needed a vacation—or how enjoyable it would be to hang out with women from the book world.

Before they returned home, they'd each tossed a message in a bottle into the ocean in hopes of finding true love. They weren't called the Romantic Hearts for nothing. Surprisingly, a few had met their dream heroes after they received replies and were now married.

Not Jenny.

She'd gone into the bottle toss with zero expectations. Oh, she'd hoped it might work out, but deep in her heart of hearts, she had a feeling it wouldn't. She might write fiction, but her life was no storybook. Her romantic past read more like a comedy—a dark one. She'd assumed a tanker or cargo ship would run over her bottle and the note would never be read. But now...

Jenny tapped on the subject line.

Message in Bottle Found
DOR2008@...
To: Jenny <8675309@...>

Message received, Jenny. I assume that's your name. 867-5309 is one of my mom's favorite songs.

Bottle found on beach in Key West.

An asteroid has a better chance of causing an ELE than an EMP. Just sayin'.

Roswell, seriously? You should be more

embarrassed about that than someone reading your message in a bottle. Guess you're a Bigfoot believer, too.

DOR

P.S. I am single and male, but not in the market for a soul mate. Hope you've found your true love.

Well, her bottle had at least reached an unmarried guy. What were the odds of that?

She laughed at his last line.

Jenny hadn't found her one true love, but that was okay. She had room for only one man in her life.

Yep, good old Ashton Thorpe.

He might only live in her mind and on the pages of her novels, but he was the ultimate book boyfriend—the kind of guy men aspired to be. Her series that featured him had made more money than she ever imagined having, and Ash would soon grace the big screen in what the producers hoped would be a successful movie franchise.

He was made for that kind of stardom... if the actor slated to play Ash could pull off his combination of courage, daring, and hotness. The right amount of swagger wouldn't hurt, either.

Larger than life was the only way to describe Ash. Perfect was another. No guy she'd dated could compete. Although... she hadn't given up hope one would someday.

Jenny read the message again. The fact DOR knew the song she used for her email address impressed her. The bottle reaching Key West didn't surprise her given the currents and the amount of time that had passed. The Roswell and Bigfoot comments brought a much-needed smile to her tired face.

Yawning, she typed off a quick reply. The cursor hovered over the send button.

Another yawn.

In the morning, Jenny would likely regret she'd responded, but she was too tired to care now. She hit send.

Will Jenny regret replying to DOR's email? If you'd like to find out what happens next, get your copy of Jenny's story!

End of Excerpt
Jenny (Beach Brides Series)
by Melissa McClone

Thank you for purchasing

CLAIR

I hope you enjoyed it!

If you enjoyed it, please consider leaving a review. Reviews help the author find readers and will help other readers find books they'll enjoy.

FICTION BY GRACE GREENE

Emerald Isle, North Carolina Novels

Beach Rental

Beach Winds

"Beach Towel" (A Short Story)

Beach Christmas *(Christmas Novella)*

Beach Walk *(Christmas Novella)*

Clair *(Beach Brides Series Novella)*

Virginia Country Roads Novels

Kincaid's Hope

A Stranger in Wynnedower

Cub Creek

Leaving Cub Creek

Other Virginia Novels

The Happiness In Between

The Memory of Butterflies (Sept. 2017)

WWW.GRACEGREENE.COM

Made in the USA
Middletown, DE
22 January 2023

22823567R00090